Claudia Talks About: Lying

I have this great new teacher—her name is Ms. Hartin. She seems to really like me, and she pays a lot of attention to me. In fact, she usually listens to me more than my own family does! Last week, I started telling her stories about my family—stories that weren't exactly true. You see, I wanted to go to this violin concert, and none of my brothers would take me. I figured if I made Ms. Hartin feel sorry for me, *she* would drive me to the concert. But it didn't exactly work out. And my family got really mad at me.

I'm Claudia Salinger. You've probably heard about my family. Everyone at school knows the story. We live alone in my house—just my brothers, my sister, and I.

My parents were killed in a car accident almost four years ago, when I was ten. That's when my oldest brother, Charlie, became our legal guardian. He's in his twenties, so I guess everyone figured he was old enough to take care of us. But sometimes he really messes things up. Like the time he forgot to pay the electric bill. We lived in the dark for a week!

But it's okay when Charlie makes a mistake. Bailey is always there to fix it. He's my other big brother. He's in college, and he's the coolest. Whenever I have a

problem, I ask Bailey for help. Like when I'm afraid I might forget how my parents' voices sounded. Or how they looked. Bailey says my brothers and sister will always be there to help me remember.

My sister, Julia, reminds me of my mother sometimes. She's really smart and pretty, like Mom was. Julia just graduated from high school. I want to be just like her when I'm eighteen!

Then there's Owen. He's only four. But I can tell that someday he's going to be a brain surgeon or something. He's *so* smart. I think he takes after me!

My brothers and sister are always busy with school or work or girlfriends and boyfriends. And I'm always busy practicing my violin. I love playing—it reminds me of my mom. Charlie says I inherited her talent. Mom used to play with one of the best orchestras in the country. Maybe one day I'll do the same thing.

Sometimes we get so busy that we don't see one another enough. That's why we eat dinner together at least once a week. We go to Salinger's, the restaurant my dad used to own. They always have our table reserved—for a party of five.

Claudia

PARTY OF FIVE™: Claudia

Welcome to My World
Too Cool for School
A Boy Friend Is Not a "Boyfriend"
The Best Things in Life Are Free. Right?
You Can't Choose Your Family
The Trouble with Guys

Available from MINSTREL Books

party of five™

Claudia

You Can't Choose Your Family

Devra Newberger Speregen

**Based on the television series
created by Christopher Keyser
& Amy Lippman**

A MINSTREL® BOOK

Published by POCKET BOOKS
New York   London   Toronto   Sydney   Tokyo   Singapore

A MINSTREL PAPERBACK *Original*

A Minstrel Book published by
POCKET BOOKS, a division of Simon & Schuster Inc.
1230 Avenue of the Americas, New York, NY 10020

A PARACHUTE PRESS BOOK

Copyright © 1997 by Columbia Pictures Television, Inc. All Rights Reserved.

Columbia Pictures Television is a SONY PICTURES ENTERTAINMENT Company.

All rights reserved, including the right to reproduce this book or portions thereof in any form whatsoever. For information address Pocket Books, 1230 Avenue of the Americas, New York, NY 10020

ISBN: 0-671-01717-9

First Minstrel Books printing November 1997

10 9 8 7 6 5 4 3 2 1

PARTY OF FIVE and its characters are trademarks of Columbia Pictures Television, Inc.

A MINSTREL BOOK and colophon are registered trademarks of Simon & Schuster Inc.

Cover photo courtesy of Columbia Pictures Television, Inc.

Printed in the U.S.A.

You Can't Choose Your Family

chapter one

Claudia? Do you know the answer or not?"

Ms. Hartin folded her arms across her chest and glared at me.

I glanced at the copy of *A Midsummer Night's Dream* that lay open on my desk. But it was no use—the answer to Ms. Hartin's question wasn't going to appear on the cover or anything. The truth was, I had no idea who the narrator of the play was.

Actually, the whole truth is I didn't even *read* the play. I wouldn't know the name of the narrator if it were Claudia Salinger.

I took a deep breath. "Um, okay, Ms. Hartin. You see, I didn't exactly finish reading the play."

Ms. Hartin just kept glaring at me.

"Well, no, that's not exactly true," I went on. "I kind of . . . didn't actually *start* reading the play. See, I had to—"

Ms. Hartin cut me off. "Never mind, Claudia," she said. She sounded totally annoyed. I watched her pick up a big red pen and scribble something inside her grade book.

Ugh. That can't be good.

Ms. Hartin snapped her grade book shut. She barely looked at me when she spoke to the class again. "Now, as you all know—well, as those of you who read the assignment last night know—Shakespeare's narrator in *A Midsummer Night's Dream* is Puck."

Puck? What kind of a name is that? I never would have guessed Puck.

I slumped down in my chair. Great, I thought. Two weeks into ninth grade and I'm already on Ms. Hartin's bad side. The worst part is that Ms. Hartin happens to be one of my favorite teachers this year. She's certainly the nicest, anyway.

I sighed. I knew this was going to happen. I knew the minute my brother Bailey flew out the front door last night—leaving me to baby-sit for my little brother, Owen. I mean, I love Owen and all. But it's impossible to get any homework done when you have to watch a four-year-old.

It's all Bailey's fault, I thought. It was *his* turn to baby-sit.

I wondered what Ms. Hartin wrote in her grade book. Probably "unprepared for class." What a way to start off the new year! I've never been unprepared for class before. My stomach began to feel weird. Now Ms. Hartin probably thinks I'm a bad student, I realized.

Something snapped me on the back of my neck. Hard.

"Ow!" I reached behind my head and rubbed my neck. Then I heard a muffled giggle behind me.

"Sorry, Claud!" a voice whispered into my ear. "I was just trying to get your attention."

I didn't have to turn around to see who it was. My best friend, Jody Lynch, sits right behind me in first-period English class. She's in my math and social studies classes, too. When she *comes* to class, that is. Jody has trouble making it to her classes sometimes. She says it's because she simply had to stop at the deli for a low-fat corn muffin. Or because she just had to run to the Gap.

It's amazing, but she never gets in *major* trouble for missing classes. Sure, she gets caught all the time. But she usually only gets detention. She's in after school detention practically every day. Jody always jokes that under her Grant High School yearbook picture it will say "Most Likely to Be Detained."

But I doubt she'll even be in school the day yearbook pictures are being taken!

Obviously, Jody doesn't care much about school. That's the biggest difference between us. I'm totally neurotic when it comes to my schoolwork.

My neck was still stinging from Jody's snap.

I leaned back in my chair. "What did you hit me with?" I whispered over my shoulder.

"Relax, Claud," Jody replied. "It was just a hair band. You'll live."

"I think I'm bleeding," I complained.

Jody snorted. "Oh, please. Spare me the melodrama. So you got a zero in the teacher's book. I'm impressed."

I knew Jody was teasing me. She thinks it's funny that I'm afraid of getting bad grades.

She's just lucky that her mother never gets on her case about her grades. Her mom doesn't get on her case about *anything*. Jody's parents got divorced when she was little, and now her mother is always too busy working to pay much attention to Jody. She pretty much lets Jody do whatever she wants. Like the time she let

4

Jody go to a concert in Los Angeles with some friends. *Overnight!*

My brother Charlie would never let me go on an overnight to another city. For an older brother, Charlie can be very overprotective. But he has to be. If he doesn't act responsibly when it comes to Owen and me, Social Services might find out. Then Owen and I could be put in a foster home or something. And I can't even think about the possibility of that happening. It would be the absolute worst thing. Ever.

Charlie is my legal guardian. Owen's, too. Our parents were killed in a car accident a little over three years ago. Charlie has been our guardian ever since. He's only in his twenties, but he's very mature. So far, I don't have any major complaints. Well, maybe he could be a little less strict when it comes to my curfew. Charlie goes nuts if I'm home even one single second late!

Charlie never gets mad when Bailey or Julia miss curfew. Well, I guess I should say he never *got* mad. My older brother and sister don't have curfews anymore. Bailey is in his second year of college. And Julia got married right after she finished high school last year. She and her husband, Griffin, live in an apartment in another part of San Francisco.

"So what's up for the weekend, Fiddle Girl?" Jody

whispered. "Want to hit the mall on Saturday? Or maybe go see a movie?"

"I can't," I whispered back. Ms. Hartin kept looking in our direction as she was lecturing, so I stopped talking.

It used to annoy me when Jody called me Fiddle Girl, but now I'm used to it. She calls me that because I play the violin. I'm really serious about it. I play in competitions and recitals all over California.

I know Jody is pretty impressed that I'm such a good violinist. Last month she even came to hear me play in a recital at UC Berkeley. It was the first time she'd ever heard me play when we weren't hanging out in my bedroom. After the concert she said she couldn't believe how awesome I was. That meant a lot to me.

When Ms. Hartin walked to the other side of the room, I leaned back in my chair.

"I can't do anything on Saturday," I explained quietly. "I'm going to a concert this weekend."

Being a violinist is great. The only problem is it doesn't leave me much time for a social life.

"Can I come?" Jody asked.

I shook my head. "I'm not playing, I'm watching," I told her. "I'm going to see this amazing young violinist who—"

"Never mind," Jody cut me off. "Maybe we can do something on Sunday. Where's the concert?"

"In Palo Alto," I explained. "It's a little over an hour away. Ross gave me the tickets."

Ross Werkman is my violin teacher. I've known him all my life—he's like a part of the family. He was planning to take me to the concert himself. But then the string quartet he plays in got a job that night.

I guess Charlie will have to take me, I thought. I made a mental note to remind him about it tonight at our family dinner.

"Claudia!" Jody whispered again. This time her voice was loud enough for Ms. Hartin to hear. She glanced over at us suspiciously. I didn't dare turn around. I had to watch it—I was already on Ms. Hartin's bad side.

"Claud!" Jody tapped my shoulder when Ms. Hartin looked away. I ignored her.

Then she started kicking the leg of my chair.

"Cut it out!" I finally whispered. "I'm in enough trouble already!"

Jody nearly choked. "Oh, please!" she whispered. *"Claudia Salinger,* Miss Straight-A, in trouble? Right!" I couldn't see her face, but I knew she was smirking.

I turned halfway around in my chair. "Jody, this is not funny! If Charlie finds out that I—"

"Claudia!" Ms. Hartin said loudly. "I'm sure you're not discussing Shakespeare's comedy, so I have to assume you aren't paying attention!"

I turned back around and swallowed hard. Ms. Hartin was glaring at me again.

"Sorry, Ms. Hartin," I muttered.

Ms. Hartin stared at me a few seconds more, then finally spoke.

"See me after class, Claudia."

I felt my heart sink to my knees. After class? Oh, no!

I rubbed my hands back and forth on the legs of my jeans. I do that when I'm nervous. Ms. Hartin kept talking about Shakespeare, but I couldn't concentrate on a word she was saying. Ms. Hartin wanted to see me after class. *Me.* Claudia Salinger. I've *never* had to stay after class to talk to a teacher.

"Ooooh, someone is in big trouble!" Jody whispered behind me. I could tell she wasn't very concerned about my current situation.

So I ignored her again.

"Come on, Claud! I'm just kidding!"

I kept ignoring her.

Jody leaned up to me really close. "Listen. Take it from an old pro. This 'after class' stuff isn't so bad."

I turned around and glared at her. Then I faced front

8

again. Luckily, Ms. Hartin was writing on the board. She had her back to us.

"Want some advice?" Jody whispered. She didn't wait for me to answer. "Stay cool. Don't crack under the pressure, and you'll be fine."

Stay cool. Oh, sure. That was easy for *her* to say. She couldn't care less about her grades.

"I'll wait right outside the door," Jody added. "When Ms. Hartin is done yelling at you, I'll be right there."

I swallowed hard. Wonderful, I thought. There's going to be *yelling.*

The bell rang. All the other kids jumped up and began heading for the door. I felt like everyone was staring at me as they walked past my desk. Another friend, Karen Jacobs, gave me a sympathetic smile. But it didn't make me feel any better.

"Right outside," Jody mouthed to me as she left.

I wasn't sure what I was supposed to do. I got up from my chair and lifted my book bag off the floor. I slung it over my shoulder and walked slowly toward Ms. Hartin's desk. She was busy reading something, so I just stood there, waiting for her to look up.

My stomach was full of butterflies. Why didn't she yell at me and get it over with? Was I supposed to say something first? Finally, I cleared my throat.

Ms. Hartin glanced up at me. "Oh. Claudia," she said with a frown. "I'd like to know why—"

Suddenly, before I could stop to think about what I was going to say, I was talking. Rambling, actually.

"Ms. Hartin, I'm sorry!" I blurted out. "It wasn't my fault! I had to baby-sit for my little brother. I know that sounds lame, but it's just me and my brothers in the house and I get stuck watching Owen a lot."

So much for acting cool.

"See, Bailey was supposed to watch Owen," I went on. "But he had a wrestling match or something and Charlie was at the restaurant and, well, I would have called Julia to come over, but she and Griffin were out or something, so I didn't have a choice."

Ms. Hartin just stared at me with her mouth hanging open.

"I had to watch Owen—so I didn't get to read the play. But I'll read it all tonight! I promise! And this will never happen again! Please don't give me a bad grade. Charlie will be mad if I—"

Ms. Hartin held up her hand. "Claudia, wait a minute!" she cried. She flipped open her grade book and started reading again.

This is weird, I thought. Now I'm back to standing here like an idiot.

When Ms. Hartin finally glanced up, her expression had completely changed. She didn't look angry anymore. She looked, well, kind of sympathetic.

"Claudia," she said in a quiet sort of voice. "I didn't realize . . . I mean, the office told me of your situation at the start of the year, but, well, I must have just forgotten."

Huh? What was she talking about?

"I was really so sorry when I heard. Such a tragedy! Losing your parents at such a young age. How are you holding up?"

Oh—she meant *that* situation.

"I'm okay," I told her. I hate when people ask me how I'm holding up. Like they expect me to be walking around crying all the time or something. I mean, I miss my parents like crazy, and I *do* cry about it sometimes. But I haven't, like, been walking around weeping for three and a half years.

"Well, if there's ever anything I can do," Ms. Hartin said warmly.

"Yeah, uh, okay," I said with a shrug. How about giving me an A in your class? I thought.

"Anyway, I'm sorry I came down so hard on you before. But promise me, in the future you'll let your family know when you have an important assignment to complete. You have priorities, too, Claudia. Your brothers and sister need to understand that."

I nodded.

Ms. Hartin smiled again. "Okay. Well, you'd better be getting to your next class."

I felt my eyes widen. That was it? No yelling? No screaming? No having to write "I will not come to class unprepared" one hundred times? Excellent!

"Okay. Thanks, Ms. Hartin!" I ran out of the classroom before she could change her mind. This was great!

Jody grabbed me as soon as I walked through the door.

"I can't believe it!" she cried. "You did it, Claud!"

I was grinning from ear to ear. "Yeah, I did it!" We gave each other high-fives, then headed for our lockers. "Um . . . what did I do . . . exactly?" I asked.

"Just brilliant!" Jody went on. "Better than any excuse I've ever come up with. Using your parents to get off the hook like that. It was perfect! I didn't think you had it in you, Fiddle Girl."

I followed Jody down the hall. Suddenly, I didn't feel so happy anymore. Was *that* what had happened?

Had I used my parents' death—to get out of trouble?

chapter two

I took a long sip of my cherry Coke, then placed the glass back down on the table. I glanced around Salinger's. The place was empty.

It's still kind of early, I thought. The dinner crowd usually comes in around six-thirty or seven.

Salinger's is the restaurant my dad used to own. Charlie runs it now. Julia, Bailey, and I help out as much as we can.

The food at Salinger's is pretty awesome. Charlie hired this excellent chef a while back. Her name is Tonya and she makes the most incredible chocolate mousse. I order it at every family dinner.

I always look forward to our family dinners. Not only because of the mousse, but because it's really the only night we get to eat together as a family. Usually, Charlie tells us what's up for the following week and what chores and stuff he needs us to do. Then Bailey tells us all about college, Julia and Griffin talk about married life, and I always try to tell at least one funny story.

But tonight I hadn't even gotten one word in—let alone a funny story. Bailey, Charlie and Julia had been arguing since we sat down.

I took another sip of my soda and sat back in my chair. Julia was still complaining. What had it been, five minutes straight already?

"No way, Charlie!" Julia insisted. "I am not driving across town every week just to do your dirty laundry!"

Charlie slapped his chores chart on the dinner table. "Keep your voice down, Julia!" he whispered harshly. "The customers can hear you!"

I glanced around Salinger's. There were only about five other people in the whole restaurant, and two of them were waiters.

"But I mean it, Charlie!" Julia replied, her voice a little quieter. "You'll have to take me off your laundry chores chart. I don't think it's fair that I have to come all the way from my apartment to the house to wash everyone else's clothes!"

I cleared my throat, desperately trying to change the subject. We'd been discussing dirty clothes for half an hour and it was getting pretty boring. Plus, I needed to talk to everyone about a much more important subject—who was going to take me to the violin concert in Palo Alto on Saturday?

"Hello? Can I say something?" I asked.

"I used to do it!" Bailey snapped. "I used to drive from *my* apartment near school to do the laundry. Just because you've moved out, Julia, doesn't mean you don't have family responsibilities."

Julia rolled her eyes. "Don't lay that on me, Bay," she replied. "I do my share! Who do you think wakes up a whole hour early three days a week to rush across town and get Owen to day care on time?"

"Excuse me?" I tried again. "Can I say something? I wanted to—"

"Come on, Julia!" Charlie put in. "Don't drag Owen into this. Would you rather he drove himself to day care in the morning?"

"Can I drive the car, Tarlie?" Owen asked with a big smile.

I laughed because Owen looked so cute, with spaghetti sauce all over his face, hands and clothes. Owen almost always eats spaghetti at our family dinners at Salinger's. It's his favorite food. Griffin caught my eye and laughed, too.

But no one else noticed how adorable Owen was at the moment. They were too busy fighting.

"Fine!" Bailey said. "You do the laundry and *I'll* take Owen to day care."

"No!" Owen yelled. "I want Julia!"

"You see?" Bailey asked. "You've spoiled him, Julia. Ever since you moved out, he won't do anything I ask him to do."

"Oh, please, Bailey," Julia said. "Owen just isn't used to you being back in the house."

Bailey had moved back home a couple of months ago. Before that, he lived in an apartment near his college. But he had a hard time living on his own—he started drinking a lot. In fact, he became an alcoholic. I mean, he still *is* an alcoholic. He doesn't drink anymore, but Bailey says that in Alcoholics Anonymous—that's the support group he belongs to since he quit drinking—they call you an alcoholic forever, even if you've stopped drinking. Bailey says he's a *recovering* alcoholic.

Anyway, he's been in AA for almost six months now and he's really doing great. But Owen still isn't used to having Bailey around all the time. Plus, since Julia moved out, we've had to shuffle all the baby-sitting duties around. Poor Owen doesn't know *who* to listen to. He's been having a lot of temper tantrums.

"Jul-i-a!" Owen yelled.

"Owen, use your quiet voice," Bailey told him.

"JUL-I-A!" Owen yelled louder.

"You guys! I have something important to say!" I tried again. "Charlie, I need—"

"Well, then if Bailey takes Owen to day care, I'll do the laundry," Julia put in. "But I'm bringing over mine and Griffin's dirty stuff, too."

"Fine," Charlie said.

"Every week," Julia added. "Even the weeks that I'm not on laundry duty. It's only fair that if I have to wash your stuff, you have to do mine and Griffin's."

"Don't drag *me* into this," Griffin protested.

"That's ridiculous, Julia!" Bailey cried. "We're not washing your dirty clothes! Our basement isn't a Laundromat!"

"Guys! Can we stop talking about the laundry for one second?" I pleaded.

"No, wait, Bay," Charlie said. "Julia has a point. If she's going to come all the way out to participate in the chores, it's only fair that she brings her stuff, too."

"And *Griffin's?*" Bailey asked.

Griffin groaned. "Jules . . ." he began.

"He's my husband, Bailey!" Julia yelled, her face red. "Get used to it! He's part of the family now!"

"Then he should be on the chores chart, too," Bailey said.

I slumped in my seat. I could see that this conversation wouldn't end anytime soon.

"Charlie!" Julia complained.

Charlie sighed. He dished some more spaghetti onto Owen's plate.

"Yum!" Owen said happily. He picked up a handful of pasta and shoved it into his mouth.

Ugh, what a mess! That tomato sauce would never come out of his T-shirt—no matter who ended up doing the laundry.

"Owen! No—don't eat with your hands," Bailey said.

Owen opened his mouth and showed Bailey a mouthful of chewed-up spaghetti.

Julia laughed.

Bailey's face turned red. "Oh, sure, Julia—encourage him!" he snapped. "Owen, listen to me. Use your fork."

Owen spit his food onto the table.

"Owen! Use your fork!" I ordered.

Owen picked up his fork. "Can I have soda?" he asked me.

Charlie lifted the pitcher of soda and poured some into Owen's cup.

"Owen shouldn't drink soda all the time," Bailey pointed out. "It's bad for his teeth."

"Since when did you become the expert on raising children?" Julia snapped. "You can't even get Owen to listen to you."

"Since I've been taking child psychology," Bailey replied. He turned to Charlie. "This course I'm taking is really cool, Charlie," he said. "I think it can help us a lot with Owen's problems."

"What problems?" I asked. "Owen doesn't have any problems!"

"Sure he does," Bailey said. "He won't do a single thing we say."

"Actually, Bay, he'll do whatever *I* say," Julia told him. "And he listens to Claudia and Charlie. He just doesn't like you!"

Bailey glanced down at his plate.

"Of course he likes Bailey!" I cried. "He's just not used to having *two* big brothers living with him."

"It's okay, Claud," Bailey said. "My psych professor

says Owen is probably angry with me for moving out and then coming back. And he's angry at Julia for leaving. So he won't listen to me, and he always wants her. It's fairly normal. Owen just has to get used to his new schedule."

"Well, he won't get used to it unless we finish coming up with a new schedule," Charlie pointed out. "So Bailey will take Owen to day care three days a week. And—"

"I think Owen just likes me better," Julia cut in. "Because Bailey is so mean to him!"

I could tell she was teasing, but Bailey got mad.

"I'm not mean to him—I just want him to do things for himself, Jules," he argued. "*You* dress him and feed him and tell him when to go potty and everything. But he's supposed to be doing those things for himself now! He's four years old!"

"So what?" I asked. "He's developing at his own pace."

"No—according to my psych class, he's slow," Bailey said. "And it's Julia's fault!"

Julia rolled her eyes. "Can we please get back to something real—like the laundry?" Julia asked.

"No!" I cried. "I have to ask something!"

"Yes," Charlie said. "Here's my final decision. I'm

going to stretch the laundry schedule to every three weeks," Charlie told Julia. "Then you wouldn't have to come every other week. You could come every third Friday, and you could bring your and Griffin's laundry with you."

"No way!" Bailey argued. He seemed to have forgotten about Owen's deep psychological disorders. "Then I'll be taking Owen to day care *and* doing the laundry for two weeks straight!"

Charlie held up his hand. "No, you won't," he explained. "You'll still be taking turns, and Julia will bring her and Griffin's stuff over only on her week. And Claudia will now be getting the added responsibility of laundry chores. She's old enough."

Huh?

"You can start this Saturday, Claud," Charlie went on. "Since Bailey has his wrestling match, and Julia and Griffin will be away for the weekend, it's the perfect time for you to start. You're baby-sitting for Owen anyway."

"I'm *what?*" I cried.

"You have to watch Owen," Charlie explained. "Because I'm training a new manager at the restaurant this weekend."

My mouth fell open. Wait a second. How had this

happened so fast? How had my life completely changed in five seconds?

"That sounds fair," Bailey said. He lifted his fork and stabbed it into his chicken marsala.

"Okay by me," Julia added, pulling apart a dinner roll and popping a piece into her mouth. "Want half of my roll, Bay?"

"Great—thanks," Bailey said.

Everyone munched and chewed on their dinner as if nothing tragic had just occurred.

"Hang on just a minute!" I said loudly.

Everyone stopped eating and looked up at me. Even Owen stopped slurping up a strand of spaghetti.

"Claudia, what is it?" Charlie asked.

"What is it?" I repeated in amazement. "What is it? I'll tell you what it is! Don't I get a say in anything? Don't any of you even think of *asking* me if it's okay to volunteer me for laundry and baby-sitting this Saturday? It isn't even my turn to baby-sit!"

"Claud—" Charlie began.

"It's always the same," I interrupted him. "Claudia will do it—no problem! Well, for your information, there *is* a problem! I can't do the laundry chores this week. And I can't baby-sit, either. I have very important plans!"

Charlie groaned. "What are you talking about, Claudia? What plans?"

"That's what I've been trying to tell you all night!" I snapped. "Don't you remember Ross gave me those tickets to see Joshua Bell in concert?"

"You have concert tickets?" Bailey asked.

"Who is Joshua Bell?" Julia asked. "I've never heard of him."

I rolled my eyes. Sometimes I wonder how it is humanly possible that I'm related to any of these people.

"He happens to be a concert violinist. One of the youngest, most talented violinists in America." I turned to Charlie. "I told you about these tickets last month, Charlie! I've been looking forward to this concert for weeks."

Charlie put his head in his hands and rubbed his eyes. "Claudia, I wish you had mentioned this earlier."

I stood up at the table, ready to explode from anger and frustration.

"Earlier?" I shouted. "I've been trying to talk about it all night! And I've been talking about this concert every day for three weeks now! How much earlier could I have mentioned it?"

"Claudia!" Charlie whispered. "Please! The customers!"

I clenched my fists together tightly. "Sorry," I muttered, lowering my voice. "It's just that I *did* tell you about the concert. Weeks ago."

"Well, I still don't think we can swing it, Claud." Charlie checked his chores chart again. "That concert is in Palo Alto, right?"

I nodded.

"Claudia, that's at least an hour away. And the concert will probably be another two hours, plus the drive back. . . . I can't leave the restaurant for that long. In fact, with this new trainee, I'm probably going to be tied up here all weekend. Maybe, if Bailey can take you . . ."

I felt my heart beating faster and faster. This wasn't looking good at all.

"Nope," Bailey said through a mouthful of chicken. "I have that wrestling match."

"Can't you go late?" I suggested hopefully.

Bailey shook his head. "No way. I can't bag out on the team. Not after I screwed up so much last year with the drinking and all."

I shot a desperate look at Julia. Surely she'd understand.

"I'd love to take you, Claud . . ." she said.

I breathed a sigh of relief. "Thanks, Jules!"

24

"But we're going away to Napa this weekend for our six-month anniversary," Griffin put in. "We already paid for the hotel."

I could not believe this was happening. How could my family just ruin this concert for me?

"Sorry," Julia added.

I felt completely speechless. A million thoughts ran through my head. Didn't I count in this family? Weren't my plans important, too?

"Does anyone see how totally unfair this is?" I finally asked. My voice cracked as I spoke.

"We're sorry, Claudia," Charlie said. "But there's nothing we can do. Maybe you can catch Joshua Bell the next time he comes through town."

"The next time he comes through town? What do you think he is, an express train? Joshua Bell doesn't appear very often! I can't believe you guys don't see how hugely important this is to me." I gave Charlie my most pathetic pleading look.

"Charlie, I *have* to go to this concert! Ross said I shouldn't miss it! It's important for me to see other young violinists. To sharpen my own skills, and to—"

"Come on, Claudia," Julia interrupted. "It's just a concert."

There was a lump the size of a golf ball in my throat.

Just a concert? Maybe to them. But to me it was something special. Something I'd been looking forward to for weeks.

I watched as everyone went back to eating dinner— like this was no big deal.

How come everyone in this family was allowed to make plans except me?

Didn't I have a life, too?

chapter three

"They were all being so unreasonable!" I cried.

Jody was walking me to pit orchestra rehearsal the next day after school. It was our first practice for the school play. "Can you believe it? Do you see what I have to put up with?"

Jody shook her head. "Totally pathetic," she agreed.

"It's so unfair!" I said for the millionth time. "Everyone in my family gets to have a life. Bailey and Julia can make whatever plans they want. And Charlie doesn't even question them! But if I ever try to make plans for something, I have to go through the third degree with Charlie. Then I have to find somebody to cover for me at home. I never get to do anything! I really have no life."

"Oh, come on, Claudia. You have a life."

"No. I don't!" I insisted. "All I have is school. And the violin. And nobody at home even cares about that anymore, either. They used to be so supportive of my playing. Now they don't care at all!"

"It's not like this is anything new, Claud," Jody pointed out. "They're just so wrapped up in their own lives."

"It's not fair!" I practically yelled. "They don't care, and they don't understand that some things are important to me. If they did, they would find a way to take me to this concert. It means so much to me! Think of everything I could learn from Joshua Bell."

"Joshua Bell. Is he the babe from the picture in the newspaper you showed me?" Jody asked. "You *could* learn a lot from him!"

I rolled my eyes. Jody is always thinking about boys. "Joshua is a master violinist—who cares what he looks like? And he started out young, like me. Even Ross said it was important for me to go."

Jody stopped at the door to the auditorium. "Here's where I get off," she said, shifting her backpack to the other shoulder. "I'll catch you later, Claud. I'm off to the library."

My eyes nearly popped out of my head. "The *library?*" Why would Jody—who hadn't see the inside of a library since kindergarten—go to the library after school?

Jody smiled mischievously. "Yes, Fiddle Girl! The library! Do you think you're the only one who has any schoolwork around here?"

I eyed her suspiciously. No way was Jody Lynch going to the library to do schoolwork.

"Okay," she confessed. "You see, there's this guy in my Spanish class who works after school at the library, and he's totally hot!"

I had to laugh. "Well, have fun," I said. "I'll see you later."

Jody nodded, then spun around and walked down the hall.

As soon as Jody turned the corner, my bad mood returned. I really didn't feel like going to orchestra. I would have liked to go home and catch Charlie before he left for the restaurant. Maybe if I begged some more, he'd agree to take off work and drive me to Palo Alto.

But I couldn't ditch orchestra. Especially not pit orchestra. Only the best musicians in the whole school get to perform for the play. And I was first violin. Mr.

Dumas, the conductor, had given me the sheet music for this semester's play—*Romeo and Juliet*—last week. I had three violin solos.

It was pretty music and all. But to tell the truth, after the *A Midsummer Night's Dream* fiasco yesterday, I was kind of sick of Shakespeare.

That's why it was funny when I opened the door to the auditorium—and saw Ms. Hartin. Somehow Shakespeare and Ms. Hartin just seem to go together.

"Hi, Claudia!" she called.

"Hi, Ms. Hartin," I replied. I was surprised to see her holding a viola and sitting in front of a music stand.

"Do you play?" I asked.

She nodded. "Yes. I taught music at another school before my transfer here last year." She pointed to my violin. "I heard you were a concert violinist," she said.

I nodded. "This is the first time I'm in a pit orchestra, though," I explained. "Ross—he's my violin instructor—thought it would be good for me to work on a play."

"I can't wait to hear you," Ms. Hartin said. "Mr. Dumas asked me to sit in with the orchestra for rehearsals. The music is just beautiful . . . have you heard it?"

I nodded.

"Where do you usually sit?" she asked, glancing at the empty chair next to her.

"I guess I can sit here," I said, setting my violin case on the chair. "Since it's the first day, I'm not really sure where to go." I lifted my violin from its case.

"Claudia!" Ms. Hartin cried. "What a beautiful instrument!"

I nodded. I'm very proud of my violin. "It used to be my mother's," I explained.

Ms. Hartin put a hand on my shoulder. "That makes it even more beautiful," she said.

That was kind of a corny thing to say, I thought. But it was nice to hear anyway.

"This is my mother," I said. I took the photograph of Mom from my case.

I always carry the picture with me. It's a photo of Mom playing with the San Francisco Orchestra exactly one year before she died. I like to look at it whenever I play. Mom and I used to practice together all the time. And when I see her picture in front of me, I can pretend I'm playing just for her.

I pulled out my bow and rubbed the rosin along the horsehair. Then I rested the violin under my chin and lifted the neck in my left hand. I raised the bow with my right hand and began my usual warm-up. When I was finished, I glanced up at Ms. Hartin.

Her mouth was practically hanging open.

"Claudia! I . . . I had no idea you were this talented. I'm very impressed. That was lovely!"

"Thanks." I smiled. "It was just a warm-up." Maybe it was the crummy mood I was in, but just hearing someone praise me for something—anything—made me feel a lot better.

"I got my talent from my mother," I added, stealing another glance at Mom's picture. "She was the most amazing musician ever."

Maybe I shouldn't have said that last part, because when I turned back to Ms. Hartin, she looked ready to cry.

"You poor thing," she murmured. "That's sweet of you to keep her picture near you when you play."

Normally, I hate it when somebody looks at me with that "you-poor-little-girl" look. But for some reason, today I kind of liked it. It was nice to have an adult interested in me for a change. I mean, no one at home cared.

When the rehearsal started, I played my very best. I

guess in some way I was trying to impress Ms. Hartin. But then, as I played my solo, I really got caught up in the music. It was beautiful. Mom would have loved it.

During the solo I could practically feel Ms. Hartin smiling next to me. Then she picked up her viola and joined me. I hadn't realized this part was a duet. A chill ran through my body.

This is almost like playing with Mom, I thought.

I hadn't felt so comfortable playing the violin in three and a half years. I closed my eyes and imagined that I was sitting with Mom in the living room, playing a duet from the classical music book Dad gave me for my tenth birthday.

A second later, the rest of the orchestra joined in. For a first rehearsal, I have to admit we sounded pretty good.

When rehearsal was over, Ms. Hartin offered to walk me to where the after-school buses waited. We talked about the orchestra, about *Romeo and Juliet,* and about the school where she used to teach.

"I conducted the high school orchestra and taught English," she told me. "I would have loved to conduct again here at Grant, but you already have a terrific conductor."

I nodded. Mr. Dumas was great.

"For fun," Ms. Hartin went on, "I joined the city orchestra. I played viola for the Palo Alto Symphony."

Palo Alto. The Joshua Bell concert.

I was going to miss it.

My bad mood returned instantly. I had almost forgotten about missing the concert. Rehearsal had taken my mind off it for a little while.

"Claudia, is something wrong?" Ms. Hartin asked.

I frowned. "It's nothing," I said. "It's just that when you mentioned Palo Alto, it reminded me of an excellent concert that I'm missing this weekend."

"You mean Joshua Bell?" Ms. Hartin asked.

I stared at her. "Yes! How did you—" Then I realized, of course Ms. Hartin would know about the Joshua Bell concert. Anyone who cared about music would know about it.

"That's the one," I muttered.

"My husband and I are taking my daughter to the concert," Ms. Hartin said. "Why aren't you going, Claudia? You really should, you know. There's so much to learn from hearing a master violinist in concert. It can help your playing. Don't you have tickets?"

"I have tickets," I said quietly. "But . . . I can't go. I

34

have some family stuff to do, and . . . well, I have to. That's all."

Ms. Hartin shook her head. She seemed even more disappointed than I was.

"You know, Claudia, someone in your family should understand how important this concert is for you to attend."

I nodded, since I couldn't think of a thing to say. She was one hundred percent right. But it didn't matter. Charlie had made up his mind. I was the family slave this Saturday.

I climbed up the four steps to the bus and waved to Ms. Hartin. Then I took a seat near the front and watched her from the window.

Ms. Hartin smiled at me. It was another one of those "I-feel-so-sorry-for-you, you-poor-little-girl" smiles. I felt a lump form in my throat. I prayed I wouldn't start bawling on the school bus. That would be the ultimate in humiliation.

Ms. Hartin is nice to care so much, I thought as the bus pulled away from school. She cares about me and about my violin.

Too bad *she* isn't part of my family.

Then I'd be going to the concert for sure.

chapter four

The next morning when I woke up, I headed straight for Bailey's room. I wanted one last chance to plead my case. I had missed Charlie last night—Bailey was my last hope.

I just had to make Bailey understand how much the concert meant to me. He always comes through for me when I really need him.

Bailey's bedroom door was wide open, but he wasn't inside. It suddenly occurred to me that I hadn't heard him come home last night. But why would he stay out all night? Plus, it was his first morning to get Owen to day care.

I walked down the hall to Owen's bedroom. I pushed

open the door. Bailey and Owen were sitting on the floor in front of a photo album.

"Okay, Owen," Bailey said. "What do you see in this picture?" He held up a photograph.

"A boat," Owen replied. "Now can I have Cocoa Puffs?"

Bailey shook his head. "No, not yet. I still have six more pictures."

"Bailey, what's going on?" I asked.

"I don't want to look at the picture book anymore!" Owen said. "Claudie, can I have Cocoa Puffs?"

I stared at the pictures on the floor next to Bailey. They were photos from an album of Bailey as a baby that Mom had put together. "What's going on?" I asked again.

Bailey sighed, as if explaining it to a mere high school student was totally beneath him.

"I'm trying to develop Owen's language skills," he said. "It's a method used on children to teach them vocabulary and to speak properly."

I rolled my eyes. "Bay, Owen is too young to do this kind of stuff."

"But he doesn't speak as well as he should at age four," Bailey insisted. "It's because he's used to being with Julia, and she finishes his sentences for him. He's never had to speak for himself."

"I want Julia," Owen whined.

I grinned. "That sounds like a complete sentence to me," I said. "Bailey, Owen has been talking since he was two. His language skills are fine."

"Maybe," Bailey said. "But he refuses to get dressed. I've been telling him to do it for fifteen minutes now. Obviously, something is troubling him."

I glanced at Owen. He sat cross-legged on the floor, resting his chin in his palm.

"The only thing troubling him is that he hasn't had breakfast yet," I said. "Julia always fed him *before* he got dressed."

"I want Cocoa Puffs!" Owen said.

"Well, I'm not Julia," Bailey said. "And I want him to get dressed first. Come on, Owen. Put your shirt on."

"No!"

"Bay, you can't change his routines all at once," I said. "Just let him get used to you first."

Bailey sighed, then put the photo down. "Yeah, okay, Owen. You can go."

Owen's face lit up. "Can I have two bowls of Cocoa Puffs?" he asked.

Bailey nodded.

"Yay!" Owen cried. He gleefully pulled a box of tissues off his dresser and tossed a handful high into the air.

"Owen!" Bailey yelled.

I shook my head. Poor Bailey was going to have his hands full with Owen.

"Owen, go fix yourself a bowl of cereal," I told him. "We'll be down in a sec, okay? I need to talk to Bailey."

Owen nodded, then raced downstairs.

"What's up?" Bailey asked when Owen was gone.

I took a deep breath. "Okay, here it goes. Bailey, this concert on Saturday is *majorly* important to me. For a lot of reasons. But most of all, Ross thinks I should go. And so does my English teacher."

Bailey frowned in confusion. "I don't get it. Why would your English teacher care if you go to a violin concert?"

"Because she's a musician, too. And she thinks I can learn a lot from going to this concert. So does Ross. That's why he gave me the tickets."

Bailey sighed. "I already told you, Claud. I can't help you. I have a wrestling match."

I was ready for that answer. "But what if you drove me to Palo Alto really early?" I suggested. "I can hang around the concert hall for a few hours until the show starts, and you can get back for your match."

Bailey laughed. "Like Charlie might ever let you hang around a concert hall all alone in another city!"

"Well, maybe Jody can come with me. I have *two* tickets," I pointed out.

"Oh, right, Claud. You know how much Charlie loves Jody—I'm sure he'll give you permission to hang around Palo Alto with *her*." He started downstairs.

Bailey was right. That was a dumb idea. Charlie isn't a big fan of Jody's. He thinks she's trouble. Actually, he's right. Jody *is* trouble, but she's also my best friend. She can be loads of fun, and really sweet, too. But Charlie doesn't see that side of her.

And why should I have to ask for his permission anyway? I'm fourteen years old! I groaned. This was just not working out, no matter what I tried.

"Come on, Bailey—I'm dying here!" I pleaded. "I really, really want to go to that concert."

Bailey stopped at the bottom of the stairs. "I know you do, Claud. And I'm sorry I can't be more of a help. But I'll tell you what. I'll try to think of something, okay?"

I plopped down on the top step and rested my chin in my hand.

Great.

He'll think of something.

Big deal.

What could Bailey possibly think of that I haven't thought of a million times already?

I pulled on the door handles as hard as I could, but the school doors were locked.

Oh, wonderful, I thought. Now I'm locked out.

This was unbelievable. I'd been running late all morning. First, I missed my usual bus because I was so busy begging Bailey to take me to the concert. And now I was late for first period.

Ms. Hartin was going to kill me.

A security guard let me in and I raced to the office. After the bell rings, you need a late pass to get into class.

The secretary gave me a disapproving look as she stamped my late pass. I snatched it away and headed down the hall to English. I glanced at my watch—seven minutes late.

Slowly, I pushed the classroom door open. Ms. Hartin was in the middle of a lecture. I slipped inside as quietly as possible. Maybe she wouldn't even notice.

She stopped talking as soon as she saw me.

The classroom grew so quiet, I could hear my heart beating. Everyone was staring my way.

This is it, I thought. She's going to scream at me!

But Ms. Hartin just went on with her lecture. I hurried to my desk and sat down.

"So anyway," Ms. Hartin said to the class, "I want you all to think about the theme of the play. What did Shakespeare have in mind when he set out to write this comedy? I'll give you a few minutes to look over the play and write down your thoughts."

I opened my notebook and pulled my copy of *A Midsummer Night's Dream* from my backpack. This was perfect. I would just slip right into the classwork as if I weren't late in the first place.

"Claudia?" Ms. Hartin said suddenly. "Can I see you out in the hall for a moment?"

My heart sank. Did I really think I could get away with coming in late? Who was I kidding?

I followed Ms. Hartin into the hallway. I hoped she wouldn't yell loud enough that the rest of the class would be able to hear.

Ms. Hartin put her hand on my shoulder. "Claudia, is everything all right?" she asked quietly.

I blinked in surprise. "Um, yeah."

"Everything okay at home?"

I nodded. "Yeah. I just missed my bus."

"Are you sure?" she asked.

"Uh, yeah, everything's fine," I replied. I wondered why she was looking at me so strangely.

"It isn't like you to show up late for class," Ms. Hartin said. "It must be because of some difficulty at home. You can tell me, Claudia."

My mind was racing. She wasn't yelling at me. She would let me off the hook if I told her I was late because of a family problem.

"I missed my bus because Charlie overslept, so *I* had to get Owen ready for day care," I lied.

Ms. Hartin's eyes widened.

Why had I just said that? I couldn't believe I lied to my teacher! But I really didn't want to get in trouble.

"And then I had to walk him to day care because Charlie was late for work," I added.

Ms. Hartin shook her head. "How did you get to school?"

"Oh—I had to take a city bus," I told her.

I didn't even know why I kept lying. I wanted Ms. Hartin to think I really had it tough. I mean, I could have just said I missed the bus. But she seemed to want me to say there was a problem at home.

Ms. Hartin gave my shoulder a little squeeze.

"You poor thing—so much responsibility on your

shoulders. It's very mature of you to take care of your little brother like that. Listen, honey, don't worry about it, okay?"

Oops. Maybe I'd gone too far. She called me honey!

I nodded. "Okay," I said. "I'm sorry I was late."

Ms. Hartin smiled again. "Really, Claudia. Don't give it another thought. Let's go inside."

Back in my seat, I breathed a sigh of relief. I couldn't believe how easy that had been!

A minute later, Jody walked through the door.

"Miss Lynch! I hope you have a good reason for coming late to my class today!" Ms. Hartin cried.

Wow. She sounded much more angry than she had when I came in. I watched Jody stare at the floor. "I missed my bus," she explained.

"That's not good enough," Ms. Hartin snapped. "I'll see you in detention after school."

Jody frowned and took her seat behind me. I was still shocked. What was going on? I had been late, too—and I used the exact same excuse! But I got a pat on the shoulder, and Jody got *detention!*

I picked up my pen and scribbled a note to Jody.

Jody—
I can't believe she freaked out on you! I was late, too.

But I didn't get in trouble. Will your mom be mad about the detention?

I ripped the note out and folded it up as small as I could. Then I put it in my hand and casually reached behind me. When Ms. Hartin looked away, I dropped it on Jody's desk.

A few minutes later I felt something slip down the back of my shirt. I groaned. I hate when Jody passes me a note like that. My T-shirt was tucked into my jeans, and now I had to *un*tuck it to get the stupid note.

It took me a few minutes, but I finally got Jody's note out of my shirt. I opened it and read.

Like my mom really cares if I get detention! No way! Anyway, I already have *detention today after school, so who cares?*

I shook my head. I guess I shouldn't be surprised— Jody has detention almost every day. But I still have a hard time believing her mother doesn't care. I read the rest of her note.

Of course you didn't get in trouble—Ms. Hartin loves you! You have this great "my-family-has-it-so-tough" thing going. She feels bad for you. I bet you can get her to do anything you want. Hey!!! Can you get her to give you the answers to our first English test???

I almost laughed out loud when I read that last part. Then I read the note again. Jody actually had a point. Ms. Hartin felt bad for me, and she was treating me differently.

That's really not fair, I thought. It's like she thinks I can't take getting in trouble because Mom and Dad died. I don't want any special treatment just because I'm, you know, an orphan!

Then I got to thinking. Maybe Jody was right. Maybe I *could* get Ms. Hartin to do anything I want. Well, not like giving me test answers or anything. But there was *something* that I wanted. Something that I could have done if Mom and Dad were alive. I wanted to go to that concert in Palo Alto.

And Ms. Hartin was already planning to go there herself. . . .

I ripped out another piece of notebook paper and began to write.

Jody—
You gave me a great idea (no, I won't ask Ms. H for

the test answers!). But maybe if I play up this family stuff enough, I can get **Ms. H** *to take me to the Joshua Bell concert!!!*

I passed the note back to Jody. A second later she tapped me on the back. I turned around to see that she was smiling.

"*Now* you're thinking like a pro, Claud!" she whispered.

I faced front again. Just then Ms. Hartin looked my way and smiled. I knew right then and there that the rest was going to be easy.

Forget Bailey and his "I'll think of something, Claud!" I would get my own ride to the concert!

chapter five

All through orchestra practice, I tried to glance at my watch.

Not an easy task when your wrist is turned the other way so you can play the violin.

Finally, I had a musical break and was able to peek. Six-twenty!

I couldn't believe it. Practice had run way, way late today. Mr. Dumas *had* warned us it might be late, but I never imagined that meant six-twenty! I only hoped Charlie or Bailey would be around to pick me up so I wouldn't have to take a taxi home. The after-school bus was long gone by now. Even the *after* after-school bus was history.

At six-thirty Mr. Dumas finally ended rehearsal. I

packed up my violin and bolted out of the auditorium to the pay phone. There was no answer at home. Typical.

I dug in my backpack for the twenty-dollar bill Charlie puts in there for emergencies. I had to take everything out and search through all my books, but finally I found it stuck in my math folder.

I called a taxi and went outside to wait on the steps. At least this would give me time to finish *A Midsummer Night's Dream.*

I was reading the last scene, when a small blue car stopped in the drive in front of me. Ms. Hartin called to me from the open window.

"Claudia! Where's your ride?" she asked. "It's starting to get dark!"

I opened my mouth to explain that I was waiting for a taxi, but I quickly changed my mind. This was a perfect opportunity to make her think my family was ignoring me—and ignoring the fact that I wanted to go to the Joshua Bell concert.

I tried to look as pathetic as possible.

"Charlie was supposed to pick me up," I lied, letting my voice crack as I spoke. "I guess he forgot."

Ms. Hartin leaned across the front seat of her car and opened the passenger door.

"Get in," she ordered.

I jumped into the front seat, trying not to smile. Operation Get-a-Ride-to-Palo-Alto was going perfectly.

I thought about the Joshua Bell concert. I was as good as there!

"Does Charlie often forget to pick you up after practice?" Ms. Hartin asked as we drove.

I nodded sadly. "I mean, I know he's busy with the restaurant and all," I said, trying to sound as if I were making excuses for him. "But he hardly ever remembers my schedule. Once, I had to walk home from my own violin recital at the university."

I could see Ms. Hartin's hand clutch the steering wheel tightly.

"That's terrible," she said. "It's very unfair for your brother to place so much responsibility on you."

"Oh, it's not *that* bad," I replied. "It's just a few chores around the house, you know, the cooking and the cleaning. Oh, and taking care of Owen and Thurber—he's our dog. Oh, right, and I almost forgot. Now I have laundry duty, too."

"You're responsible for all that, Claudia?" Ms. Hartin asked as she pulled the car onto my street.

I pointed to my house and she turned into the driveway.

"Yeah," I said. "But it isn't so bad. I can still fit in my homework before I go to bed. At *eleven-thirty.*"

I didn't mention that Charlie always tries to make me go to bed earlier. Or that I stay up that late only to watch TV. I was hoping she'd think I was like Cinderella or something—like I couldn't start my homework until all my chores were done.

Ms. Hartin stared at me. I opened the door and got out of the car.

"Thank you so much for the ride," I told her. "It's nice to have someone listen to me for a change. No one here ever has any time for me." I pointed a thumb toward my house.

I turned to walk to my front door. That was great, I thought happily. She must think I'm really in need of attention!

Suddenly I heard a car door close behind me.

"I'm coming inside with you, Claudia," Ms. Hartin called.

"Huh?" I asked in surprise. "Why?"

"I want to make sure someone is home," Mrs. Hartin said. "I'm not going to leave you here alone."

I gulped. "Well, okay," I said nervously.

Maybe I shouldn't have said those things about my family. I mean, Ms. Hartin would be able to tell that I *don't* come from a neglected home as soon as she got inside.

I opened the front door and Ms. Hartin followed me in.

We didn't have to walk far into the house to know there were people home. In fact, from the sound of things, there were a *lot* of people home.

"Come on," I told Ms. Hartin. "They're in the kitchen. I'll introduce you."

Ms. Hartin nodded. I took one step toward the kitchen—and felt warm liquid splatter around my shoe.

"Oh, yuck!" I cried. I looked down at the puddle I'd stepped in. It was pale yellow.

"Hey! Didn't anyone walk Thurber today?" I yelled out.

Just then, Owen flew by us. He was completely naked.

Bailey ran after him. "Owen!" he cried. "Come back here and get dressed!"

"Hi, Claudie!" Owen stopped to stare at Ms. Hartin. "Is she a mean lady or a nice lady?"

I noticed Ms. Hartin's eyes widen.

"She's nice," I assured him.

"Owen! Come get dressed!" Bailey yelled again. Owen ran into the living room with Bailey on his heels.

"What's going on?" I asked.

Nobody answered me.

Charlie stormed out of the kitchen. He barely glanced at me. I frowned. He looked really angry. And really *tired*. Come to think of it, I hadn't even *seen* Charlie since the other night at the restaurant. I wondered if he'd been at Salinger's ever since.

"Bailey!" he shouted. "What happened to Owen's spare clothes? He's supposed to have a change of clothes at day care in case he has an accident!"

"Owen had an accident?" I asked. That was strange. He's been toilet trained for ages.

Bailey shouted back from the other room. "He used the spare clothes yesterday when he jumped in that mud puddle. It took me so long just to get him dressed this morning that I forgot to pack more spare clothes."

"Bailey—how could you do something like that? Owen had to sit around for an hour in wet clothes this afternoon," Charlie cried. "When I picked him up, he was soaking wet!"

Bailey came into the room, carrying Owen. It was amazing. He and Charlie were having this argument, and neither of them had even realized I was standing in the room. With a *stranger!*

"Listen, Charlie," Bailey said. "Julia never made Owen

dress himself. And it's about time he learned how. I spent a long time teaching him how to put on a shirt. It's more important than remembering his spare clothes. I don't want him to be slow in his development."

Charlie ran a hand through his hair in frustration. "You're the one who forgot to pack his spare clothes!" he yelled. "I think *you're* slow in your development!"

"Put me down!" Owen yelled. "I don't want you to hold me!"

"No, Owen," Bailey snapped. "You have to get dressed."

"NO!" Owen began to cry.

I stole a glance at Ms. Hartin. She stared at my brothers with her mouth hanging open. I tried to smile, as if this kind of stuff happened in our house all the time.

"Um, Ms. Hartin, why don't we go in the kitch—"

"SHUT UP! I mean it, Griffin! Just shut up!"

Before I could even *point* to the kitchen, Julia came stomping out of it, followed by Griffin.

"Oh, come on, Julia. You're overreacting!" Griffin replied angrily.

"Really?" Julia asked. "How is it overreacting? I'd really like to know! You go and spend *our* money on something useless and—"

"Hey!" Charlie interrupted. "Can you two take it someplace else? I'm trying to deal with Owen here!"

Julia ignored him. "We worked hard for that money," she went on, "and you don't even think about asking me—"

"Julia!" Owen yelled. He squirmed around so much that Bailey had to put him down. He ran right over and threw his arms around Julia's leg, sobbing the whole time.

Julia scooped him up in her arms and hugged him. She turned to Bailey. "Why don't you stop yelling at Owen all the time, Bay?" she cried. "He's just a little kid!"

"Don't attack Bailey just because you're mad at *me,*" Griffin put in.

"Stay out of this, Griffin!" Julia snapped.

This is a total nightmare, I thought. I glanced up at Ms. Hartin.

She seemed so stunned by my crazy household, she looked like a stone sculpture. I figured I really ought to say something. At least alert the rest of the family there was a teacher here.

"Uh, hello?" I said. "Does anyone even realize I'm home?"

Charlie stopped yelling for two seconds. "Claudia,

weren't you supposed to arrange dinner tonight?" he demanded.

Oops. I *knew* something had slipped my mind!

"Um, yeah, but orchestra practice ran really long this afternoon and I couldn't. Should I call for pizza or something?"

"Never mind," Bailey said. "I already did."

Just then, Owen sneezed.

Charlie threw up his arms. "You see!" he cried. "Now he's sick! That's what happens when kids sit around in wet clothes, Bay. Now I'm going to have to take a day off tomorrow to take him to the pediatrician!"

"Charlie, if you weren't such a workaholic, you might see that your priorities are really messed up. My psych professor says therapy does wonders for—"

"That's what we need, Griffin! Marriage counseling, I swear! How you get off thinking you can just spend money we don't have on stupid little—"

"Julia, Griffin," Bailey said to them. "Can you stop fighting in front of Owen, please?"

Owen sobbed even louder.

"Bailey!" Julia screamed. "Just get off my case. It's not *my* fault Owen doesn't want to listen to you!"

"I don't want to get dressed!" Owen yelled. "I don't want Bailey!"

"It's okay, O," Julia soothed him. "You don't have to get dressed now."

"Nice job, Julia," Bailey said. "Now he'll never do a single thing I tell him to."

"Will both of you just stop it!" Charlie yelled.

"No, Charlie. *You're* the one who should be getting Owen dressed tonight, anyway," Bailey cried. "You're so irresponsible!"

I stared at my family in shock. Suddenly I felt embarrassed. I mean, I'd wanted Ms. Hartin to think we were troubled—but not *this* troubled! Did my brothers and sister even see how ridiculous and immature they were being?

Ms. Hartin finally found her voice. She leaned over and whispered in my ear.

"Claudia. Please . . . I'd love it if you came to my house for dinner. I can bring you back later."

I took one last look at my family, who were *still* yelling and bickering. I really don't even think they knew I was home.

"Sure," I said. "Anything is better than this place."

I followed Ms. Hartin to the front door and stepped outside.

"I'm leaving!" I shouted to anyone who was listening. Somehow, I doubt anyone was.

chapter six

You listen to music during dinner?" I asked Ms. Hartin.

I still couldn't believe it. Here I was, sitting at a nice, calm dinner table with no fighting, bickering, or vegetable-throwing.

And classical music was playing in the background.

Ms. Hartin laughed as she carried a serving dish to the table. "Sure," she replied. "Don't you like to listen to classical music? You must like hearing violin pieces, at least."

"I love to!" I told her. "But the only music Owen ever lets us play on the stereo downstairs is Barney."

Keri, Ms. Hartin's seven-year-old daughter, giggled. "Hey, Claudia," she said. "Can I braid your hair?"

"Keri," Ms. Hartin said, "maybe Claudia will let you braid her hair *after* we've eaten dinner."

"Oh, okay," Keri replied.

I smiled at Keri, but I couldn't help feeling a little jealous of her. I remember when I was seven. Mom *always* wanted to braid my hair. But I hated it! I thought I looked like Pippi Longstocking or something. My hair was a lot longer then—almost halfway down my back.

Now I'd give anything to have Mom around to braid my hair again. Maybe I'll let Keri braid it tonight, I thought. I mean, if I hated it, I could always take it out later.

"Okay! Who's hungry?" Mr. Hartin came into the dining room carrying a big bowl of food. He placed it on the table and my stomach growled when I saw what it was.

Chinese food!

A great big bowl of chicken, broccoli and peppers over rice. It looked and smelled delicious.

"You *made* this?" I asked Ms. Hartin.

She laughed. "Nope. Mr. Hartin is the cook in our family. I couldn't hard-boil an egg without instructions!"

I laughed. "Well, it looks excellent, Mr. Hartin. My

father was a great cook, too," I added. "He used to fill in for the cook at Salinger's all the time. That's the restaurant that my family owns."

Suddenly, everyone got quiet. I guess it was because I'd mentioned Dad. I saw Ms. Hartin exchange a worried look with her husband. I guess she told him about my parents' death.

Time to change the subject, I decided.

"We don't get to eat such great meals at home anymore," I said. "Charlie has been spending every minute at the restaurant lately."

"Doesn't Charlie cook dinner for you?" Ms. Hartin asked.

"Oh, yeah, right!" I fibbed. "If you can call heating up a TV dinner cooking." I felt a pang of guilt as I said that. Actually, Charlie is an amazing cook. He inherited it from Dad, I think.

Charlie makes incredible dinners. His big thing is "theme night." He picks a kind of food, like Italian, and then he makes a huge meal of entirely Italian food. But he hasn't had time to do that in a while.

"That's terrible," Ms. Hartin said, shaking her head.

I glanced up—and saw her looking at me with this sad, sympathetic expression on her face.

Well, maybe I shouldn't feel guilty about complaining, I thought. I mean, Charlie *has* been at the restaurant all the time lately.

And besides, if Ms. Hartin felt sorry for me, she would definitely offer to take me to the concert!

"Yeah, usually *I* end up cooking for me and Owen," I added.

"Do you eat TV dinners every night?" Keri asked.

"Not every night," I told her. "Sometimes Bailey takes care of dinner for Owen and me."

"Can he cook?" Mr. Hartin asked.

I laughed out loud. "Oh, please! Bailey—cook? No way. But he's great at ordering pizza."

"So you eat *pizza* every night?" Keri asked in amazement. "That's so cool!"

"Not exactly," I told her. "Only when Bailey is home. He has AA meetings two or three times a week. On those nights it's just me and Owen and a box of cereal."

Mr. Hartin coughed. He raised his eyebrows and glanced at Ms. Hartin.

Oops. Maybe I'd gone too far, mentioning Bailey's drinking. I guess seven-year-olds don't really need to hear about things like that. And I didn't even mean to bring it up—it just sort of popped out.

"Bailey goes to Alcoholics Anonymous meetings?" Ms. Hartin asked nervously.

I stared down at my plate. Bailey would *kill* me if he knew I'd just broadcasted his personal life over dinner.

I ignored Ms. Hartin's question. "So you can see why I'm so impressed with this dinner, Mr. Hartin," I said, trying to sound cheerful. "It's really delicious! I haven't had a good, home-cooked meal outside of Salinger's in . . . well, in a long time."

I picked up my fork and shoveled in a heap of chicken and rice. This really *was* delicious! Julia used to cook Chinese food for us all the time at home, but it never came out this good.

"What about your sister?" Ms. Hartin asked. "Who was that she was, uh, *with* at your house before?"

I put down my fork. "Oh, Griffin?" I asked. "He's Julia's husband."

Ms. Hartin's eyes widened. "But . . . she seems so *young!*" she said in surprise.

"Yup. She is," I said, lifting my fork again. I took a big bite of broccoli and chewed. "She's eighteen. She got married a few months ago and moved into Griffin's apartment. You should have seen Charlie after Julia told us she'd gotten married! Boy, was he *mad!*"

"I'll bet," Mr. Hartin said.

"Well, he's not mad anymore," I added. "Just when Julia and Griffin fight, like they were doing at the house before. They do that a lot. Can I have some more chicken?"

Mr. Hartin didn't move for a second. Then he realized he was the one closest to the bowl of chicken. "Yes. Of course. Take as much as you want. I can even pack you up some to take home," he added. "For Owen."

I smiled. "Great! Thanks!"

They were all staring at me as if I were some kind of injured bird or something. It felt a little too weird. I mean, my family isn't *that* unusual. Maybe I should just talk about the concert, I thought.

"Anyway," I went on. "They all have their own problems, so it's no big deal to them if I miss the Joshua Bell concert. Even if it is a *really* big deal to me. Lots of times I seem to get lost in the shuffle. But I would give anything to go to that concert!"

I leaned over my plate again and started eating my second helping of dinner. Then, from the corner of my eye, I saw it—Ms. Hartin and Mr. Hartin nodded at each other.

Bingo!

"Claudia," Ms. Hartin said.

I looked up and stared at her with the sweetest, most innocent face I could make.

"Yes?"

"Why don't you come to the concert with us?"

I gasped—but not *too* dramatically. Ms. Hartin can probably spot acting from a mile away.

"Really?" I asked. "Go with you?"

Ms. Hartin smiled and Keri clapped her hands. "Wow, Mom! Really? Can Claudia come with us?"

Ms. Hartin looked at me.

"Claudia?" she asked. "How about it? Will you come with us?"

Ladies and gentlemen! Children of all ages! Behold Claudia Salinger—the greatest actress the world has ever seen!

I smiled gratefully.

"Definitely!" I replied.

chapter seven

It was almost nine o'clock when Ms. Hartin dropped me off back at home. I couldn't wait to tell everyone the good news!

Unfortunately, no one was even around to tell. It was weird—when I'd left before, the place was a zoo. Now it was as calm and quiet as a museum. Nothing to show how nuts it had been a few hours ago, except for the empty pizza carton on the kitchen table.

I went up to my room and opened my copy of *Macbeth*. I didn't have to have it read for another two weeks, but I thought I'd get a jump on it anyway. Ms. Hartin had said it was one of her favorite Shakespeare plays, so I figured I'd check it out and see what she meant.

I was just getting into it, when I heard Charlie's car door close in the driveway. I raced downstairs just as Charlie, Bailey and Owen walked in through the front door.

"Hey!" I said cheerfully. "Guess what?"

Charlie glared at me. "You know, Claud, you forgot to leave us the phone number of where you were tonight."

I folded my arms across my chest. "I *told* you I was going to Ms. Hartin's for dinner. It's not my fault if nobody was paying attention to me."

Bailey tried to help Owen off with his jacket. "Still, Claud . . . we were nervous."

"Well, I'm home, aren't I?" I said. How dare they be upset with me? It was *their* fault for not paying attention to me in the first place. "Where were you guys?"

"We drove Julia and Griffin home," Charlie replied. "Their car wouldn't start."

"Are they still fighting?" I asked.

Charlie shrugged. "Who knows. Anyway, where were you? Did you eat?"

I nodded. "Yup! And it was great! Mr. Hartin—he's Ms. Hartin's husband—cooked this amazing Chinese stuff with water chestnuts and everything. He cooks almost as well as Dad."

"Who is Ms. Hartin?" Charlie asked.

I rolled my eyes. "Come on, Charlie! Did you hear anything I said tonight? She's my English teacher!"

"The teacher who thinks you should go to that violin concert?" Bailey asked. He was still struggling with Owen, who didn't want to take off his coat.

"Uh-huh."

Suddenly Owen began singing "Five Little Ducks" at the top of his lungs. Only it was coming out like "five wittle ducks."

"Owen, quiet down. Use your inside voice," Charlie said. "I'm talking to Claudia."

"See?" Bailey put in. "Did you hear him say 'wittle'? He always puts w's where l's are. His language development is delayed. It's because Julia was always talking baby talk to him."

Charlie groaned. "Will you leave him alone already? His language development is just fine. Stop blaming everything on Julia. Please, just bring him upstairs and get him ready for bed, okay?"

Bailey shook his head and lifted Owen up. "Come on, bro," he said gently. "Let's sing that song I taught you in the car. Ready? Little rabbit foo-foo—"

"I don't want to sing that anymore!" Owen complained as they headed up the stairs. "I want Julia to put me to bed."

When they were gone, Charlie started straightening up the living room, picking up Owen's toys and clothes from the floor. I bent down to help.

"So, guess what?" I asked again. I couldn't wait to tell Charlie about Ms. Hartin taking me to the concert. I didn't even have to make him feel guilty for not driving me.

"I can't guess, Claud. I'm too tired. Just tell me."

"Okay. Well, remember that concert I told you about? The one in Palo Alto that nobody can take me to?"

Charlie nodded.

"Well, I found someone to take me! Someone responsible! An adult!" I grinned triumphantly.

Charlie's eyes narrowed. "Who?"

"Ms. Hartin!" I announced. "My English teacher. She plays the viola and she and her husband are taking their daughter to the concert. She said I can go with them!"

Charlie stared at me as if I'd told him I was riding a rocket ship to the concert.

"It's all arranged and everything," I added. "Isn't that great?"

"Oh, it's all arranged?" he asked, sounding annoyed.

Not exactly the reaction I'd expected.

"Uh, well, yeah," I replied. "They're going to pick me up early tomorrow morning so we don't hit traffic on the bridge and—"

"Claudia, you should never have made plans with your teacher to go to that concert," Charlie said. "I already told you that you couldn't go."

I felt as if I'd been kicked in the stomach.

"What do you mean?" I asked. My voice cracked a little. "You didn't say I couldn't *go* to the concert. You only said you couldn't *take* me there!"

Charlie sighed. "And who's supposed to watch Owen tomorrow, huh?" he asked.

This is not happening, I told myself.

"And what about the laundry?" Charlie added. "You're on the chart for tomorrow. It's all been settled already, Claudia. You knew that!"

"But I told you guys I had this concert, and you ignored me!" I protested. "And I already made plans with Ms. Hartin!"

"Well, you'll just have to call her and tell her you can't—"

"No!" I shouted. "I'm not calling Ms. Hartin! I'm *going* to that concert, Charlie! I never agreed to watch Owen or do the laundry! *You* decided for me!"

"Claudia—"

"Forget it! I'm going! Why shouldn't I be able to make plans and do things like you and Bailey and Julia can?" My voice was getting louder and louder, but I didn't care. I was *mad*.

"Why do you always think, 'Oh, Claudia will do it. Oh, Claudia can take care of that.' Without even asking my opinion? I *have* an opinion, Charlie!"

"It isn't like that all the time—" Charlie began.

I didn't let him finish.

"Well, it's not fair, Charlie! I'm old enough to have opinions and make my own decisions. I'm not the family slave—you can't just throw my name on the chores chart without asking me first! I'm sorry, but one of you guys will just have to cancel *your* plans for tomorrow and baby-sit for Owen and do the laundry. Because I'm going to that concert!"

I didn't wait to hear what Charlie said next. I didn't want to—so later I could say, "Well, I didn't *hear* you say I'd be grounded if I went to the concert." Instead, I spun around and stormed up the stairs. I marched into my room and slammed the door.

"Claudia! Come down here and talk to me!" Charlie yelled from downstairs.

"There's nothing to talk about!" I shouted back. Then I slipped on my headphones and snapped on my stereo. I put the volume way, way up and lost myself in an Itzhak Perlman CD.

I didn't care to hear what Charlie had to say.
I fell on my bed and listened to the Perlman.
I was *going* to that concert.
Whether Charlie liked it or not.

The next morning I spent a whole hour going through my closet for the most perfect outfit to wear to the concert. Finally, I decided on a white button-down shirt over a pair of flowy, wide-leg black pants. I slipped on my favorite black clogs, and I looked pretty cool. Unfortunately, I didn't have a matching pocketbook or anything, so I had to carry my stuff in my backpack. It didn't exactly go with the outfit, but what else could I do?

Charlie was reading the newspaper when I walked into the kitchen. I ignored him and grabbed a breakfast bar from the pantry.

"Claudia, you're really causing big problems by not watching Owen today," Charlie said angrily.

I didn't answer.

"We're shorthanded at the restaurant, and I can't take off because the new manager is still training."

"So order Bailey to stay home. You're good at that," I snapped.

"He can't, Claudia! He's the captain. That means he's responsible for the whole wrestling team."

"Well, I'm responsible for enriching my future career as a concert violinist," I said. "And to do that, I must go to this concert!"

"Claudia, don't force me to forbid you from going. Do the right thing and call your teacher. There's still time to cancel—"

A car horn honked outside. I peeked out the window and saw Ms. Hartin's car.

"No, there isn't time to cancel," I said. My voice was shaking. I had never openly gone against Charlie's wishes before. It made me feel sort of panicky inside. What would he do to me when I got back tonight?

I picked up my backpack and headed for the door.

"Claudia! If you leave, you're grounded for a month!" Charlie shouted at me.

"So what?" I replied. "It will give me time to catch up on all my chores!"

"Claudia—get back here!"

I slipped out the door and shut it quickly behind me. Then I raced to the car and hopped in the front seat next to Ms. Hartin. Mr. Hartin sat in the back with Keri. As we pulled away from the house, I could see Charlie in the doorway. I felt like I was in a getaway car or something.

Please just drive away before he comes outside, I prayed.

Ms. Hartin pulled out of the driveway and headed down the block. I leaned back against the seat and tried to relax. My body was trembling and my heart was racing. This wasn't easy. I hated knowing that Charlie was mad at me. I don't know how Jody can take getting in trouble all the time—it was the worst!

"So, Claudia," Ms. Hartin said a few minutes later, "are you excited about the concert?"

I nodded. I *was* excited about the concert—even though fighting with Charlie had taken most of the fun out of going.

He's such a jerk, I thought. I can't believe he's ruined this concert for me—and I'm not even there yet!

"Charlie is mad that I'm going," I said suddenly.

Ms. Hartin glanced at me. "Why?" she asked.

I clenched my fists. "Because he just lost his number-one baby-sitter!" I replied angrily. "He's all mad because there's no one to watch Owen today, and now he has to do it."

Ms. Hartin took a deep breath. "Well, your brother Charlie should know he shouldn't put so much responsibility on the shoulders of a young girl."

"Yeah!" I said. "It isn't the first time, either, you know. Once, he had this girlfriend who he let move into our house! She was running for city council, and she took over the whole house. It was just me and Owen at home then. Bailey was—" I almost said "drinking" but managed to stop myself in time. I didn't want to bring *that* up again. I'd been feeling guilty about it all night.

"—he wasn't around," I went on, "and Julia was with Griffin all the time. Charlie spent every second helping Grace with her campaign, and I had to watch Owen practically twenty-four hours a day!"

Ms. Hartin was quiet.

"Well, I don't care if he has to miss work today!" I went on. "I don't care if he has to close the restaurant! It's *my* turn to do something I want to do. Let everyone else take care of the family responsibilities for a change!"

Ms. Hartin finally spoke.

"Claudia, I don't want you to worry about a thing today, okay? We're going to have a lovely afternoon. Things at home will get better. I *promise.*"

I turned to face Ms. Hartin. *Things at home will get better?*

That was a weird thing to say.

I opened my mouth to ask her about it, but I wasn't sure exactly what to ask.

So I turned back to stare out the window. What had she meant by that, "Things at home will get better"?

chapter eight

That was totally *amazing!*" I declared. "More than amazing! *Unbelievable!*"

Ms. Hartin and I stood outside the theater, waiting for Mr. Hartin and Keri to get the car. I closed my eyes and played the last few minutes of the concert over in my mind. It was awesome. Joshua Bell's fingers moved like magic. I had never seen anything like it before.

"That will be you someday, Claudia," Ms. Hartin said.

I opened my eyes and gazed at her. Had she just compared me to Joshua Bell?

"Do you really think?" I asked.

Ms. Hartin nodded. "Joshua is more seasoned than

you, but he's also older. And you both have the same passion for playing."

That was probably the biggest compliment anyone had ever given me. I smiled at her. I was really lucky to have Ms. Hartin for a teacher. Most teachers didn't bother making friends with their students this way.

I began to feel a little bad about having lied to her to get her to take me to the concert.

Ms. Hartin peered out into the parking lot in front of the concert hall. "We're supposed to meet Mr. Hartin over by that crosswalk," she said.

I followed her along the walkway, playing Mendelssohn's Violin Concerto again in my head. I opened the plastic bag I was carrying and took out my new Joshua Bell CD. I couldn't wait to listen to it on the car ride home.

"Claudia!"

I spun around—and my eyes nearly popped out of my head. Charlie stood on the sidewalk in front of the concert hall!

"Charlie!" I cried. "What are *you* doing here?"

"Come with me, Claudia," Charlie ordered me.

"But how did you—"

"I'm not asking you again. You come with me now, or you'll be grounded for a *year!*"

76

"You ought to be ashamed of yourself!" Ms. Hartin interrupted.

I thought she was talking to me, but then I realized she was looking at Charlie.

"Excuse me?" Charlie said.

"I said, you ought to feel terrible for the way you're treating your sister!" Ms. Hartin's face was red with anger, and she had stepped in front of me as if to shield me from hearing what she had to say.

"What do you mean by that?" Charlie asked. I peered around Ms. Hartin and saw Charlie's face. He looked completely shocked.

"Claudia is a *child!*" Ms. Hartin went on. "She is not old enough to handle the huge load of responsibilities you've dumped on her!"

"Hold on. Who do you think you are?" Charlie's voice shook with anger.

"A proper guardian would never leave such responsibilities to a fourteen-year-old!" Ms. Hartin went on. "You're irresponsible, immature and definitely not fit to be the guardian of two children!"

"Wait a second," I cried. "Ms. Hartin, you have it all wrong. I never meant that Charlie wasn't a proper guardian. I just meant—"

"Listen," Charlie said, cutting me off. "I don't know

who you think you are talking to me this way, but this is none of your business. Claudia is none of your business! Now, if you'll excuse me, I'm taking *my* sister home! Claudia, come *here!*"

I stepped out from behind Ms. Hartin and walked toward Charlie. My legs were shaking—I was sure they would buckle under me.

How could this have happened? I never dreamed Charlie would follow me here, or get into a fight with Ms. Hartin. I wanted to say something—to shout at Ms. Hartin for talking to Charlie like that. But I couldn't. If I did, then it would come out how I'd lied to her in the first place. She would never forgive me. And Charlie would *kill* me.

"Mr. Salinger, you're wrong about one thing," Ms. Hartin called after us. "Claudia *is* my business. As her teacher, it's my duty to make sure her home situation is secure and safe."

"Safe?" Charlie repeated. "What are you talking about? What do you know about our home life?"

Uh-oh. Here it comes! How could I have said all those awful things about my family? How would I ever be able to face Ms. Hartin again when she found out I lied to her?

78

"I know enough!" Ms. Hartin replied. "And that's why I left a message with your caseworker at Social Services yesterday."

Social Services? I stared up at Charlie. He had a look of total horror on his face.

I think I stopped breathing for a second. *Ms. Hartin called Social Services?* This was bad.

After Mom and Dad died, Social Services tried to split my family up. They said that Charlie was too young to be our guardian. That he wasn't fit to take care of us.

It had taken months to convince them that Charlie *was* a proper guardian. But that was a long time ago. I had almost forgotten that Social Services could still split us up.

But they could. And they would—if they decided Charlie wasn't a good guardian.

Charlie turned to me.

"Claudia, is this what *you* want?" he whispered.

"No! No, Charlie! I—"

"Claudia doesn't know what's best for her," Ms. Hartin cut in. "And after everything she'd told me about her family situation, it was the only thing I could do."

I felt as if I might get sick. What was going to happen?

How could Ms. Hartin have gone and called Social Services? Now they would have to reopen our file or something. All the meetings and arguments would start again. . . .

Charlie took my hand. "Let's get out of here," he said.

I followed Charlie toward the parking lot. He didn't let go of my hand. He was walking real fast, and I had to jog to keep up with him. My head was spinning.

"Charlie—" I started to say.

"Don't, Claudia," Charlie said. The look on his face scared me.

How could this have happened?

I should never have told Ms. Hartin all those stories about my family. Stories that weren't true at all.

My stomach lurched, and I almost *did* throw up.

This was all my fault!

Charlie had Julia's car. We climbed in and he began to drive in silence. I stared out the window. All I could think about was the first time I ever heard of Social Services.

It was a few days after Mom and Dad's accident. Dad's best friend, Joe, was staying at the house with us while we tried to figure out what to do. That's when we got the phone call from Social Services.

I was only ten, and I didn't really understand what

was going on. All I remember was the look on Charlie's face when he hung up the phone.

He was *crying.*

I had never seen my brother cry before. Not even at Mom and Dad's funeral. I mean, I know he *did* cry because he used up like a million tissues, but he wore these really dark sunglasses the whole time so nobody could see his eyes.

But after his phone conversation with Social Services, Charlie didn't have sunglasses on. And his eyes were red and filled with tears. I remember that it really scared me.

Charlie sat us all down that night and told us that Social Services wanted to take Owen and me away to live with some family in Sacramento. I remember *that* perfectly—it was the worst night of my life. I just sobbed and sobbed. Charlie held me tight and smoothed back my hair. He promised he wouldn't let anything like that happen.

In the end, Social Services had agreed to make Charlie our guardian. But I remember how hard Charlie had to work to convince them to let us stay together.

Was that what we were up against again? I wondered. I felt so guilty. Things had been going along so well . . . and I'd gone and ruined everything.

I think we drove for a whole hour before Charlie finally spoke to me. His voice was calm but strange. Like he was nervous but wanted to hide it.

"Claudia," he began, "you need to tell me everything you told your teacher. What did you tell her about our family?"

I choked back the tears. "Charlie! I'm so sorry! I never meant for this to happen—never!"

How could Charlie ever forgive me for what I'd done? I'd lied about my family—just so my teacher would feel sorry for me and drive me to a concert.

"Please don't hate me, Charlie."

"I don't hate you, Claud. But this is really serious stuff here. What did you tell Ms. Hartin? And more important . . . *why?*"

I took a deep breath. Charlie was going to *kill* me. Oh, why had I said all those bad things about my family to Ms. Hartin? Why?

"See," I began slowly, "I really wanted to go to this concert. And when nobody could take me, I got upset. Very upset."

"Go on," Charlie urged.

"Well, at school, Ms. Hartin was paying a lot of attention to me. She seemed to really care about me because she thought I had it tough at home. And she was planning to go to the concert herself. That's when I thought, maybe if I seem really pathetic, she'll offer to take me with her."

I stole a quick look at Charlie. He kept staring straight ahead at the road, listening. I thought maybe he'd say something, but he didn't.

"Anyway, I kind of had to seem *really* pathetic, so I sort of told Ms. Hartin that you made me take care of Owen all the time . . . and that we never ate dinner like normal families, and that Bailey was in AA and Julia and Griffin—"

That's when Charlie stopped me.

"You told her that Bailey was an alcoholic?" He looked away from the road for a second to stare at me in disbelief.

I nodded slowly. "Well, I didn't mean to. It just sort of came up while we were talking. It didn't seem like *such* a big deal. . . ."

"Claudia, didn't you think it was stupid to tell a teacher our personal family stuff?" Charlie demanded.

"No, I didn't think about that!" I replied. "Look, nobody ever has time for me at home, and here was this really nice lady offering to cook for me and listen to me and—and spend time with me!"

I felt a tear slip down my cheek. I couldn't help it. I

really had liked Ms. Hartin paying attention to me. But I never expected it to end up like this.

Charlie could hardly control himself. "But that's why I've been breaking my neck training a new manager for the restaurant!" he cried. "I wanted someone to take over my shifts so I could spend more time at home with you and Owen!"

I swallowed hard. "Really?" I asked.

"Yeah, Claud," he replied. "I know it's been crazy lately, but with Julia out of the house and Bailey back in, we had to do some major readjusting. But it's only for a short time. Things would have been back to normal soon."

Would have been.

"And now they'll never be, because of what I did, right?" I asked sadly. "Charlie, what's going to happen? Did I ruin our lives forever?"

Charlie pulled the truck into our driveway. He didn't answer me.

Oh, no, I thought frantically. Charlie won't say it, but I really *did* ruin all our lives! What if Social Services comes to check up on us because of Ms. Hartin's phone call? What if they decide Charlie *is* unfit to take care of Owen and me?

Will we be taken away?

My eyes filled up with tears again. I looked at Charlie. He kept staring out the windshield even though the car was off. All I wanted was for him to hug me and smooth back my hair the way he always does when I'm upset about something. All I wanted was to hear him say "Don't worry. I'll take care of everything."

But he didn't do any of that. He just kept staring silently into space.

"I never meant for any of this to happen!" I cried again. "I swear!"

"I know," Charlie said quietly.

"But everything's going to be all right?" I said. "Right, Charlie?"

Charlie sighed. "Sure, Claud. Everything will be fine." His voice sounded hollow. I don't think he even believed his own words.

He got out of the car and walked toward the house. I followed him.

We hadn't even reached the front steps, when the door swung open. Bailey stood in the doorway, his eyes wide and fearful.

My heart stopped. I hadn't seen that look in Bailey's eyes since the night we heard that Mom and Dad had been in an accident.

"Bailey, what's wrong?" Charlie asked. "Is it Owen?"

"There's a woman here," Bailey replied. "She's waiting for you in the living room. Her name is Sondra Turner."

Charlie frowned. "Sondra Turner?" he repeated. "Should I know her?"

"Charlie," Bailey said, "she's a caseworker from Social Services."

"Oh, no!" Charlie gasped.

"She said something about a serious complaint filed against you," Bailey added. "She's been asking a lot of questions and—"

"What have you told her?" Charlie asked urgently.

"Nothing! I told her you'd be home soon. Charlie, tell me what's going on!" Bailey's voice sounded frightened.

"You want to know what's going on?" I choked through a batch of fresh tears. I was really crying now. Hard.

"Social Services is here to take Owen and me away!"

chapter nine

I folded my hands on my lap and sat as quietly as I possibly could. I knew my face was a mess from crying, but I couldn't think about that now. I had to concentrate on what Ms. Turner and Charlie were talking about. There was a lot at stake here.

My life and Owen's life, to be exact.

Bailey sat right next to me, holding Owen on his lap. Bailey seemed as freaked out as I was. Charlie had asked us to sit on the sofa and watch Owen while he spoke with the caseworker.

He told us not to say a word. He said he would do all the talking.

I only hoped he would find the right things to say. Things that would get us out of this mess.

"Oh, um, okay, I can tell you more about that," Charlie was saying to Ms. Turner. He cleared his throat nervously. I could tell he was forcing himself to smile. Smile and pretend everything was fine.

"See, I work nights at the restaurant. At *our* restaurant, Salinger's—the one my dad owned. Okay, anyway, lately I've been training a new manager, so—"

"Mr. Salinger, please answer the question!" Ms. Turner snapped. "Why haven't you been providing meals for Claudia, aged fourteen, and Owen, aged four?"

My stomach did a somersault at her question. I couldn't believe I told Ms. Hartin that Charlie didn't feed us. Was that really what I'd said?

Charlie swallowed. He cleared his throat again.

This wasn't going so well.

"N-no, I *do* provide meals," Charlie stammered. "It's just that on the nights I work, my brother Bailey takes care of the meals."

Ms. Turner turned to Bailey. "Okay, let's talk about Bailey. As I understand, you are currently under treatment for alcoholism?"

Bailey's eyes widened. He glared at me as if to ask, "How does she know this stuff?"

A small sound escaped from my throat. Ms. Hartin had told them about Bailey's drinking! He would never forgive me for this. And I could tell that it made us look really bad to Social Services.

"Ms. Turner," Bailey said, "I've been in AA for months now, and I haven't had a drop of alcohol. My sponsor says I'm doing fine."

"Fine?" she repeated doubtfully. "But you *are* an alcoholic, right?"

Charlie came to Bailey's rescue. "Listen, Ms. Turner, you have to know that maybe things don't always fall into perfect place around here, but we're really trying. We love and support one another and—"

Just then the front door swung open and smacked into the wall with the loudest *whack* I'd ever heard.

"Charlie!" a voice screamed through the house.

We all froze. Julia.

"Charlie! I can't believe you took my car without telling me! Charlie! Where are you?"

I gulped. "Uh, we're in here, Julia!" I called back, trying to sound as sisterly sweet as possible.

Julia marched in, totally oblivious of the fact that someone else was in our living room, and that Charlie, Bailey and I were terrified.

"Charlie! Do you know what you made me do? Thanks to you, I drove all the way over here in a rented car, with a mechanic—and my car was gone! Griffin and I were supposed to leave for the weekend three hours ago!" She stopped yelling. "Uh, who are *you?*"

It's about time, Julia, I thought. I wondered how long it would take before she noticed Ms. Turner.

"Sondra Turner. And you are?"

Julia gazed around the room. "What's going on?" she asked Charlie.

Charlie didn't answer her. Instead, he turned to Ms. Turner. "Ms. Turner, this is my sister, Julia. Her car died yesterday and—"

Ms. Turner cut him off.

"Julia, do you currently live in this residence?"

Julia shook her head. "No, I live downtown with my husband. What's going on. Who are you?"

"She's with Social Services," Charlie explained.

Julia's eyes widened.

"Do you live here?" Ms. Turner asked again.

"No!" Owen yelled. "No! No! No! She doesn't live here anymore!" He burst into tears.

"Owen! Not now," Bailey whispered.

Owen scrambled off Bailey's lap and ran over to Julia.

He threw his arms around her. His face was so flushed, it was practically purple.

Uh-oh, I thought. Here it comes.

Owen screamed. I mean *screamed*. He wasn't even saying any words—he was just yelling.

What's wrong with him? I thought frantically. He hasn't had a temper tantrum like this in two years!

Julia quickly knelt and gathered him in her arms. "Owen, shhh," she said. "It's okay."

"No!" Owen screamed. He pushed her away. He looked around at the rest of us, as if trying to decide who to run to. Then he threw himself on the ground and began screaming again.

I couldn't move. Why was Owen doing this? How could he be screaming in front of Ms. Turner? What would she think of us?

"Owen," Bailey cried. He jumped off the couch and rushed over to Owen. "You're too old for this kind of behavior," he said sternly. "You need to be a good boy now."

Owen screamed louder.

"Oh, like that will really help, Bailey," Julia snapped. "You're just making him even more upset."

"Stay out of this, Julia," Bailey argued. "It's your

party of five: Claudia

fault he's like this! You always babied him, and I'm not going to do that!"

"So you'll just yell at him and tell him to grow up—that's good, Bay." Julia rolled her eyes. She took Owen's arm.

"Leave me alone!" Owen yelled. He pulled away from her.

"Look—you've totally turned him against me, Bailey!" Julia cried. "I hope you're happy now."

"Are you crazy? He's been angry at *me* ever since I moved back home," Bailey replied. "And I think it's because of you!"

"Will you both just shut up?" Charlie yelled. "I can't believe you're fighting about this! Just *shut up!*"

Everyone got quiet. Even Owen.

Charlie looked horrified, as if he had just realized how loud he was yelling.

Ms. Turner reached for her briefcase and began putting her pad away.

I watched Charlie's face. I think he was afraid to speak.

In fact, I think *everyone* was afraid to speak. Nobody said a word. The silence was unbearable.

Finally, I couldn't take it anymore. Someone had to say something. Something to convince this woman that we weren't the messed-up family she thought we were. Someone had to tell her it was all just a big mistake.

And it had to be me. After all, I was the one who had gotten us into this mess in the first place.

I took a deep breath and tried to control my voice. "Ms. Turner," I said, "the reason you're here is a mistake. A *huge* mistake. See, I told my English teacher all this stuff about my family—but it wasn't true. Not any of it!"

Ms. Turner stared at me. The expression on her face barely changed. She looked as if she heard this kind of thing all the time. As if I were making up an excuse or something.

"Really!" I cried. "Nothing I told Ms. Hartin was true! Well, okay, maybe *some* of it was true, but I told her those things only because I wanted something from her. I wanted a ride to a concert in Palo Alto and no one would take me and—"

I knew I was babbling. I wondered if I was even making any sense. As I was talking, Owen got up from the floor and ran over to Julia.

"Julia," he cried, "my tummy hurts."

"Owen! Hang on a second," she whispered to him. "We have to talk to this lady for a minute. Okay?"

"No!" Owen whined. "My tummy hurts!"

Bailey reached over to touch Owen's forehead. At that same second Owen threw up on the floor. Then he started to cry again.

"I've had enough," Charlie snapped. He scooped Owen up. "Claudia," he added, "call Dr. Belsky. Come on, O, let's go take a bath."

"I don't want to take a bath!" Owen screamed. "I'm all better now!"

I stole a glance at Ms. Turner, who was watching all this with the same stony expression.

"Owen, you need a bath!" Charlie insisted.

"No!" Owen shouted. "No bath!"

"Let me take him," Bailey offered.

"No!" Owen screamed.

"I'll take him," Julia said. "Bailey will just upset him even more."

"How dare you say that?" Bailey demanded.

"No! I don't want Julia!" Owen yelled.

I looked at Ms. Turner, who was putting on her jacket. This was a disaster.

"Let *me* take Owen upstairs," I said. "Charlie, why don't you finish talking to Ms. Turner?"

Charlie handed Owen to me, but Ms. Turner was already heading for the door. She glared at Charlie as if to say, how can you possibly control your household, when you can't even control your toddler.

"That's all right," she said. "I've seen enough." She reached into her purse and pulled out a card. She handed it to Charlie.

"I'm scheduling a follow-up visit for Monday evening," she said coldly, "after everyone has . . . calmed down. I expect you all to attend. Julia, your husband should be there as well. The address is on the card. Do not be late."

chapter ten

Dr. Belsky says he probably ate too much candy or something," I explained to Bailey and Julia. "And that he was overexcited from his tantrum. He says to just give Owen some water and put him to sleep."

"That sounds wrong," Bailey said. "I think Owen is really sick."

I shrugged. "The doctor said to call back if he develops a fever."

"Maybe we need a second opinion," Bailey said.

"Oh, now you're a doctor as well as a child psychologist?" Julia snapped. "Owen just ate too much. It's no big deal."

"Well, you shouldn't give him candy all the time,"

Bailey pointed out. "It's not healthy and it's bad for his teeth!"

"Don't worry, Bay," Julia retorted. "Now you have him so upset, he won't listen to me *or* you."

Obviously they weren't going to stop fighting anytime soon. Charlie had taken Owen upstairs to clean him up. I didn't know what to do. I had to talk to somebody about everything that was going on. But who?

I trudged upstairs and locked myself in my room. Then I called Jody.

"What's up, Claud?" Jody asked. "You sound terrible."

"I'm *worse* than terrible," I told her. "My whole life is a mess."

"Hang on! Slow down and tell me what happened."

I told Jody all about how my plan to get a ride to Palo Alto had totally backfired. About how Charlie had driven there to pick me up and how Ms. Hartin had let him have it. I also told her about Social Services.

Jody knew how serious this was. She knew all about the problems my family had with Social Services after Mom and Dad died.

"Wow, Claud," she said, "what are you going to do?"

"I don't know," I replied. "But in less than two days we have to go to Social Services and be, like, evaluated or something. And the way Owen acted today, they probably think we have no idea how to raise a little kid. What do you think I should do?"

Jody was quiet for a second. "Maybe you can talk to Ms. Hartin," she suggested. "Beg her to call Social Services again and withdraw her complaint against Charlie or something."

I considered that. It was a good idea . . . but I was sure Ms. Hartin wouldn't do that.

"I don't know," I said. "If you had seen Ms. Hartin's face this afternoon . . ."

"Well, she's the one who started this whole thing," Jody pointed out. "She's the one who called Social Services in the first place."

"Yeah, but I'm the one who gave her reason to call them," I reminded her. "I made it seem like Owen and I were raising ourselves! And now this Ms. Turner woman probably thinks it's true."

"Still," Jody said, letting her voice trail off. She was quiet for a few seconds. "Give me a day to think about this, Claudia," she said. "I promise I'll come up with something by Monday morning, okay?"

"Yeah, okay," I replied.

But I wasn't getting my hopes up.

* * *

98

On Sunday night I fluffed up my pillow for the zillionth time, then glanced at my alarm clock.

It was eleven forty-five and I wasn't the least bit tired. In fact, I was wide awake. Wide awake—and scared. Tomorrow we had to go to Social Services. Tomorrow I would find out just how much trouble I had caused.

I got out of bed and grabbed my violin case. I tiptoed down the hall to the stairs. It was pretty quiet—Charlie and Bailey were probably asleep already. I made my way downstairs and stopped in the kitchen for a bag of pretzels. Then I opened the door to the basement and walked down the steps.

Sometimes, when I'm feeling sad or depressed, playing my violin helps me feel better. Actually, I think it really just makes me forget what's making me sad in the first place—for a little while, anyway. It also reminds me of my mother, which cheers me up.

And boy, did I need some cheering up right now.

I opened the case and took out my violin. Then I rested the photo of Mom on the table so I could look at it while I played. I don't usually practice in the basement, but it was late and I didn't want to wake anybody up.

It's funny, but when I picked up the bow and nestled the violin under my chin, I couldn't think of anything to play. So I just started fiddling around and soon I was playing the overture to the *Romeo and Juliet* score.

The music was beautiful, but it didn't make me feel better. All it made me think about was Ms. Hartin and how I'd told her all that stuff about Charlie and Bailey and Julia.

I started feeling worse and worse. Especially when I looked at Mom's picture and thought about how I'd lied about my family. About my brothers and sister, who love me.

All for a dumb concert.

A single tear trickled down my cheek and splashed onto my violin. Mom would be so disappointed in me.

"I'm sorry, Mom!" I whispered. "I'm sorry for what I did. But I don't know what to do now. I don't know how to make everything right again."

I sniffled. I'd never had a problem that playing my violin couldn't help. I'd never felt so frightened and miserable before. Not since my parents died, anyway.

Carefully, I put Mom's picture and my violin back in the case and headed upstairs.

The light was on in the kitchen. Maybe I left it on when I got the pretzels, I thought. Then I noticed Charlie sitting at the table.

"Charlie?" I said quietly. "I didn't know you were up."

Charlie didn't answer me right away. First he cleared his throat.

"Charlie?" I asked again.

"Yeah, Claud. I—uh, I couldn't sleep, so I came down to . . . think. I heard you playing. It was pretty, Claud."

"Thanks," I said.

"It always makes me think of Mom when I hear you play," Charlie said. "It used to make me feel better when I listened to Mom, and it's the same thing with you."

"It didn't make me feel better this time," I confessed. "It just made me feel like I had let Mom down."

Charlie reached out and took my hand. "I don't think there's any way you could ever let Mom down, Claud," he told me. "No matter what."

"Charlie, what's going to happen to us?" I asked. "They can't really take Owen and me away, can they? I mean, they have to see that Ms. Hartin was all wrong . . . don't they?"

Charlie shrugged. "I don't know, Claudia. Her accusations were pretty serious."

I fell into the seat next to Charlie and stared into space. How had things gotten so out of hand?

"I can't believe I said the things I said," I told Charlie. "It never even occurred to me that Ms. Hartin would think you're a bad guardian. Because you're a *good* guardian, Charlie," I added. "I just never even thought that anyone would doubt that."

"Things look different to outsiders," Charlie replied. "I know I'm not as organized or as responsible as Mom and Dad—"

"Nobody expects you to be!" I cut in. "You're only one person, and you've never been a parent before! It's not fair to say you're unfit just because you're busy a lot!"

Charlie ran his hand through his hair. "I wanted to be home more for you and Owen," Charlie said. "I was trying to work it out."

Charlie looked so young right then. I get mad at him a lot, but the truth is, I never thought about how hard it must be for him. He has to work, raise Owen, and keep the rest of us together. And he does a pretty good job of it.

"I don't care what Ms. Hartin thinks," I told my big brother. "I think you're a great parent for me and Owen. I think Mom and Dad would be proud of you."

Charlie gave me a weak smile. "Thanks, Claud."

"Maybe Ms. Turner will have a change of heart tomorrow," I suggested hopefully.

Charlie chuckled. "That woman *has* no heart," he replied.

"That's for sure," I said. "But maybe, if we put on our best behavior, we can show her that we're a good family and that you're an excellent guardian. Then . . . then . . ."

I couldn't bring myself to say it out loud.

"What, Claud?"

My eyes filled up with tears. "Then Owen and I won't be taken away!" I cried.

Charlie put his arms around me and hugged me tight.

"Don't think about that, Claudia," he whispered. "But there's something I want you to know. That no matter what happens to our family, I love you."

His voice sounded funny.

"And," he added, "I'll always be there for you."

I glanced up and in the dim light I could see Charlie's eyes.

My big brother was crying.

chapter eleven

"What are you doing here?" I asked Jody.

I don't know how I managed it, but at seven o'clock the next morning I climbed onto the early school bus. I guess I just got sick of lying in bed, waiting for the sun to come up. I hadn't slept at all.

Jody got on the bus at the next stop. I couldn't believe it—Jody rarely makes the *regular* bus to school in the morning, let alone the early bus. The early bus is for kids who have sports or music practice in the morning, like me.

Jody made a face. "Duh? I'm going to school, Claudia!"

"I can see that," I said. "But why the early bus?"

Jody fell into the seat next to me. "I'm here to help,"

she said. "You sounded so awful the other night. And you look pretty awful today."

"This is helping?" I asked.

"You could really use a little blush, Claud," Jody said.

My hand went up to my cheek. I must have looked terrible. I knew my eyes were puffy and red from crying. I don't usually wear makeup, but maybe I *should* put some on today.

"Do you have any blush?" I asked.

Jody reached into her bag and pulled out a compact. She opened it and brushed some onto my cheeks. "I have a plan," she said.

"You do?" I asked.

Jody nodded. "Well, not a plan exactly," she told me. "Just an idea. I was thinking about your problem all day yesterday, and no matter what I thought, it always came back to Ms. Hartin. You have to talk to her, Claudia. Right away!"

"But she's the one who called Social Services to complain!" I reminded her.

"Right!" Jody said. "So she should be the one to call and *un*complain!"

I thought about that. Jody had a point.

"They would have to drop the investigation," Jody

said. "If there's no complaint, then there's nothing to investigate!"

Jody made it sound so easy. Like it just might work.

"What do I say to convince her she's wrong about Charlie?" I asked as the bus pulled up in front of school.

"I don't know," Jody admitted. "I think you just have to tell the truth."

"I hope it works," I muttered.

We got off the bus and headed toward school. I would find Ms. Hartin and ask her—no, *beg* her—to call Social Services.

But would she do it?

I crossed my fingers and headed for the teachers' lounge.

I waited outside the door to the lounge for a whole minute before I got up the courage to knock. When I did, the door flew open and my social studies teacher, Mr. Gerald, stuck his head out.

"Oh, hi, Mr. Gerald," I said. "I was looking for Ms. Hartin. Is she here yet?"

"Hi, Claudia!" Mr. Gerald said. He smiled at me. "Sure. Just wait a second and I'll tell her you're here. Did you get a lot of studying done this weekend?"

"Studying?" I asked in confusion. I had no idea what he was talking about.

Mr. Gerald grinned. "Cute, Claudia! You expect me to believe my best student forgot about the semester's first quiz?"

Yikes! My social studies quiz! I'd *totally* forgotten about it! At least I had a study hall period right before lunch today. I only hoped fifty minutes would be enough time to go over the entire Civil War.

"I'm just kidding!" I said, managing a laugh. "Of course I studied."

"Great. Now hang on and I'll get Ms. Hartin."

I smiled again, but I had a sick feeling in my stomach. As if I didn't have enough to worry about today, now I had a quiz to study for. How am I going to survive until our Social Services appointment tonight? I wondered.

"Hello, Claudia," Ms. Hartin said. She stood in the doorway to the lounge. She seemed uncomfortable. I wondered if she was even sorry about what had happened.

"Ms. Hartin, I *really* need to talk to you," I said.

"Claudia, I—"

"*Really!*" I pleaded. "Only for a few minutes. Please!"

Ms. Hartin nodded. "Okay, Claudia. Why don't you come in and we can talk in the conference room."

I followed Ms. Hartin through the teachers' lounge toward a large room at the other end. I'd never been in the teachers' lounge before. I tried to appear casual, but it was hard with all those other teachers there.

I wondered if Ms. Hartin had told them all about my situation. Did she tell them she thought Charlie was a bad guardian? I hope not. I avoided eye contact with anyone and walked into the conference room. Ms. Hartin closed the door.

"What is it, Claudia?" she asked gently.

I took a deep breath. Now that I was actually talking to Ms. Hartin, I was speechless. All I could do was stand there and blink.

"Claudia?"

Finally, I found my voice. "Ms. Hartin," I said. "I . . . I made a terrible mistake!"

I burst into tears. I couldn't stop myself. Just the thought of being taken away from Charlie and Bailey was more than I could stand.

"Claudia, honey, calm down. Please! Now, tell me . . . did Charlie do something?" She passed me a box of tissues.

I blew my nose. "Huh?" I asked.

"Because I can alert Social Services if he's done anything . . . to hurt you," Ms. Hartin said.

Hurt me? *Charlie?* Was she serious?

"Ms. Hartin!" I exclaimed. "Charlie would *never* hurt me! He loves me! He takes care of me! I'm not here to *complain* about him."

"Then why are you here, Claudia?"

"Ms. Hartin, it's all *me*," I said. "This whole mess. It's all my fault."

Ms. Hartin's eyes narrowed. "Claudia, you can't blame yourself for your brother's lack of responsibility."

"No!" I cried. "Charlie's not irresponsible. He didn't do *anything* wrong! He's not a bad brother and he's not a bad guardian. He's great—he's the best guardian!"

"But you told me—" Ms. Hartin began.

"I know," I interrupted her. "I know what I told you."

I took a deep breath. It was time to explain. Get it all out in the open.

Time to confess.

"It all started last week when I wasn't prepared for class," I began. "When you wanted to see me after class."

"I remember," Ms. Hartin said.

"Okay. Well, I was a little surprised when you let me off the hook so fast—after you realized I was the one whose parents died."

"I didn't let you off the hook, Claudia," Ms. Hartin protested.

"Yes, you did," I replied. "But it's okay. I'm used to getting that reaction from people. When somebody hears about my parents, they always feel sorry for me. See, I really *did* have to baby-sit for Owen that night. But most nights I *don't* baby-sit. Most nights I just do my homework and watch TV or something."

Ms. Hartin looked confused. "What are you saying, Claudia?"

"I'm saying that on that morning my excuse was for real. But I made up some other story because I didn't want to get in trouble. I *never* get in trouble at school." I lowered my head. Confessing like this was *really* hard.

"What do you mean?" Ms. Hartin asked.

"Well, that night I got into a fight with Charlie," I explained. "Because he couldn't take me to the Joshua Bell concert. Then you started being so nice to me. And when you said you were going to the concert . . . I, well, kind of thought that it would be cool if I could get *you* to take me."

110

Ms. Hartin put her hands on her hips.

"So I started making up all these stories," I went on. "Trying to get you to feel even more sorry for me." My heart began to beat faster. I stared at the floor again. I couldn't look Ms. Hartin in the eye.

"I just got carried away, that's all!" I was crying again, but I didn't care. This entire misunderstanding was my fault, and I had to own up to it.

"I told you things about Charlie that aren't true. Not one bit! I mean, he *always* makes Owen and me dinner. He makes sure I get to school on time and he spends all his free time with Owen. And he's usually very fair about letting me do things."

"Claudia—"

"And the other stuff I told you," I rushed on. "About Bailey's drinking and Julia getting married—I shouldn't have told you those things. They were private matters in my family. But you were being *so* nice . . . and I *really* wanted to see Joshua Bell . . ."

"Claudia, if you're saying these things now to cover for your brother—"

"No!" I cried. "I'm not. I made all that stuff up. Charlie usually works only one or two nights a week. And he's the *best* guardian. He helps me with homework, even when he's got a million other things to do. And he cares about Owen so much. He even visits him at day care every afternoon for lunch!"

Ms. Hartin didn't say a word.

So I kept on talking. "And, yeah, Julia's a little young to get married, but she and Griffin really love each other. And okay, we all fight and complain . . . but not more than any other family! We love one another."

I know I was talking *very* fast, but I was on a roll and couldn't stop.

"You know, even when Bailey was drinking—we didn't desert him. We tried to help him! And he's been sober for so long now. You have to understand, Ms. Hartin. I was making things sound worse than they are only to make you feel sorry for me. And to get a ride to the concert."

Ms. Hartin was staring at me as if she'd never seen me before. "Claudia," she began.

"Wait!" I interrupted. "I just want to say one more thing."

Ms. Hartin sighed. "Go ahead," she said.

"I know what I did was wrong. *Very* wrong. And I'm really, really sorry." I tried to swallow over the huge lump that was stuck in my throat. I wiped my eyes and grabbed another tissue. "You were so nice to me, and it really was cool to have someone pay attention to me. . . . But I should never have lied to you."

"Claudia, what do you want me to say?" she asked.

I looked up at her through my watery eyes. "Please, Ms. Hartin," I begged. "Don't let Social Services take me away from my family. They're the only family I have left! I love them, and I want to stay with them. I know what I said before, and how I told you it was so rough on me at home, but it's not true. I love living at my house with my brothers."

"Claudia, I understand what you're saying," Ms. Hartin said. "But you may be just a little too young to know what's best for you right now."

"But I *do* know what's best for me!" I protested. My voice cracked. "Staying with my brothers! It's what my parents would want for me."

Ms. Hartin didn't answer.

"Please!" I cried. "Please do something to help me. Take back your complaint against Charlie. *Please* help me!"

Ms. Hartin opened the door to the conference room. She stared at me for a moment, then spoke.

"Claudia," she said. "You may not realize this right now, but I *am* helping you. Social Services needs to assess your home situation. Now, the first bell is about to ring, and we both have to get to class. Why don't you visit the girls' room first and get cleaned up? We can finish this discussion later if you'd like."

I stood there, blinking at Ms. Hartin in complete shock. Discuss this later? I thought. When? After Owen and I are living with some family in Sacramento?

I began to tremble as I followed Ms. Hartin out of the conference room and through the teachers' lounge. How could she be so cold? I wondered. Didn't she see what she was doing to me? To my family?

I stood in the hallway in a daze long after Ms. Hartin had left.

"Claudia!" Jody called from down the hall. She ran up to me with a worried expression on her face. "Wow! What happened in there? You look awful."

I dried my eyes with the back of my sleeve. "It was a disaster," I said. "A total disaster! Even after I poured my heart out, Ms. Hartin still thinks Social Services should be involved."

"No way!"

"She . . . she doesn't even care if they take Owen and me away from Charlie!"

I didn't want to go to Ms. Hartin's class right now. I didn't think I could stand it. And I didn't want to start bawling there in the hallway, either.

"Listen, Jody," I said. "I can't stay here today. I'm going home. Will you talk to my teachers for me? Get my homework assignments or something."

Jody made a face. "Yuck, really?" she asked.

I nodded. "Especially Mr. Gerald. We have that social studies quiz today. Tell him I went home sick. It's not really a lie."

"Of course I will," Jody said.

"Thanks." I headed toward the doors.

"Claud?" Jody called after me.

I turned around.

"What?"

Her face was serious. "Are you going to be okay?" she asked.

"I don't know," I replied.

And that was the truth.

chapter twelve

Come on, Owen, tie your shoe!" Bailey pleaded.

"No. Want Julia to tie it!" Owen cried.

"Leave him alone, Bay," I said. "Just tie it for him."

"He should be doing these things by himself already!" Bailey insisted. "Just because Julia spoiled him doesn't mean *I'm* going to. He has to realize that I do things differently from Julia."

"Will you drop that already?" Charlie asked. "I can't listen to you guys fight today. It's bad enough that we all ended up screaming at each other in front of Ms. Turner. I don't want to do it again here."

"I'm not going to fight with Julia," Bailey promised. "But he has to get used to taking care of himself without her. Come on, Owen . . . first you cross the laces—"

"I don't want to!" Owen whined. "I want to go home!"

I could see Bailey was getting frazzled, so I stepped in. I smoothed my brown skirt under me and sat in the seat next to Owen.

"It's okay, Owen," I said gently. "We all wish we were home right now. But we have to go inside that office first."

Owen yawned. "Why?" he asked.

"Because we have to talk to that . . . *nice* lady who came over the house last night," I told him.

I hated to call Ms. Turner "nice," but I didn't want Owen to know how I *really* felt. He might accidentally repeat something in front of her. Kids are like that.

Owen started to cry. "Claudie, I don't want to go in there! I want to go home!"

I put my arms around him and gave him a big hug. I felt so bad for him. The outer lobby of a dingy office building at Social Services was no place for a four-year-old to be at eight o'clock on a Monday night.

"Okay, how about this?" I said, smiling. "If you stop crying, we'll go for ice cream afterward. Even Julia and Griffin."

Owen stopped and looked up at me. "Can I get a rainbow pop?" he asked.

"Sure!"

Bailey rolled his eyes. "Bribery isn't going to help in the long run, Claud," he complained. "And where is Julia, anyway?"

"Right here, Bay!" Julia snapped as she pushed through the lobby door. "And just because you can't control Owen is no reason to yell at Claudia."

"*You* should talk!" Bailey replied. "You're the one who got Owen so spoiled in the first place."

"You guys . . ." Charlie said.

"Right. No fighting," Bailey answered. "So where is Griffin? The caseworker said he should be here."

"He *will* be here!" Julia said. "He had to work late. Some people work for a living, Bailey!"

Charlie stepped between them. "Guys, we're supposed to be on our best behavior here, remember? This is serious! Our lives depend on what happens in the next hour."

Everyone grew quiet immediately.

My stomach gave a loud growl. I had purposely skipped dinner because I thought if I ate something, I might throw up from nervousness.

"Salinger?" a voice called from the front office. A short man with a mustache gazed in our direction. We all stood.

"Yes. We're the Salingers," Charlie told him.

The man looked us up and down. "Very well," he said. "Come in, please."

We all followed Charlie into the office. My knees grew weaker and weaker as I walked. It was like going to a new school on the first day. I didn't know *what* was going to happen in there.

I read the name on the office door as I walked inside. MR. MERRY—FAMILY SERVICES it said.

Mr. *Merry?* If the situation hadn't been so scary, I would have laughed. This was about the most *un*merry place I'd ever been.

Inside, there were two chairs behind a big desk. Ms. Turner sat in one of them. She looked as unpleasant as she had on Saturday. Worse, even.

The guy with the mustache—who I guessed was Mr. Merry—sat in the other chair. He didn't look as scary as Ms. Turner, but it was hard to tell by his expression because his mustache was so big. It pretty much covered his whole mouth and a lot of his chin.

On the other side of the desk there were four chairs set up. I figured they were for us. We all took a seat and I let Owen sit on my lap. Griffin will just have to stand when he gets here, I thought. *If* he gets here.

When we were all sitting, Mr. Merry cleared his throat and began.

"My name is David Merry," he said. His voice was flat and serious. I could tell Mr. Merry was all business.

"And I'm the head of the Family Services division of San Francisco. You already know the caseworker assigned to this case, Sondra Turner. Please be advised that this is hereby a formal inquiry into a serious complaint filed against Mr. Charles Salinger. It will be our decision, after this interview, on whether Claudia Salinger and Owen Salinger should be allowed to remain in his custody."

I froze. I shot a look at Charlie, who seemed just as surprised. This was going to be a *formal inquiry?* I'd thought this was just going to be another round of questioning!

A wave of nausea rushed over me. This was far more serious than I'd imagined. These people were already considering taking Owen and me away from Charlie.

And this meeting was going to be the deciding factor!

I didn't think I would last through the meeting. I felt sick to my stomach.

Just then Griffin walked into the office.

"Who are you?" Mr. Merry asked.

Julia stood up. "This is my husband, Griffin Holbrook," she said.

Mr. Merry and Ms. Turner exchanged glances.

"Yes, please come in," Mr. Merry said. "You'll have to stand, though, since there aren't any more chairs."

Griffin shrugged. "Okay," he said.

Mr. Merry opened his mouth to speak, when suddenly Owen began to shout. "I want Griffin to tie my shoes!"

Oh, no, I thought. Not again. Please don't let Owen act up again.

I glanced at Charlie. He looked panicky.

"Owen, just come here, I'll do it, okay?" I whispered.

"No! I want Griffin!"

Bailey looked at Mr. Merry apologetically. "I'm sorry," he said. "But it's past his bedtime."

"Go ahead, Owen," Charlie said. "You can go to Griffin."

Owen hopped off my lap and went over to Griffin, who bent down and laced Owen's sneakers.

That was close, I thought. Maybe Owen will be quiet now.

Mr. Merry began again. "The procedure in this formal inquiry is—"

"I have to go to the potty!" Owen suddenly cried.

Mr. Merry sighed.

"Owen, now isn't such a good time," Charlie said quietly.

"Please?" Owen asked.

"Oh, okay," Charlie said. "I'm sorry, Mr. Merry . . . Ms. Turner, but I *have* to take him."

Mr. Merry and Ms. Turner exchanged glances again. "There's a bathroom out in the hall," Mr. Merry said. "Two doors down."

"Great. Thanks." Charlie reached for Owen, but Owen pulled away.

"No!" he said loudly. "I don't want to go with you!"

I could see Julia squirm in her seat. I knew what she was thinking—Owen was going to have another tantrum right there in the office.

"Do you have to go or not?" Charlie asked. I don't know how he could sound so calm.

"I have to go," Owen insisted.

"He'll let me take him," Julia said. "I always take him." She held out her hand to Owen.

"No!" he yelled.

Julia looked shocked. She opened her mouth, but no words came out.

I had to do something—and fast.

"Okay, O—I'll take you," I offered. "Let's go."

Owen stared up at me for a minute, as if he were thinking about it. "No," he finally said.

He glanced around the room, staring at each of us thoughtfully.

Ms. Turner gave Mr. Merry a meaningful look. It was a look that said This toddler doesn't trust any of his siblings. I felt like crying.

"Please, Owen?" I begged. "Come with me?"

"No."

"Owen, would you like me to take you to the bathroom?" Ms. Turner asked.

I saw Charlie, Bailey and Julia turn to stare at her in horror. Then we all looked at Owen. What if he said yes? Would they think he'd rather be with a total stranger than with us?

"No!" Owen yelled.

I breathed a sigh of relief.

Griffin stepped forward. "Hey, buddy," he said. "How about me?"

Owen looked at him. Then he nodded. Griffin took his hand, and they headed for the doorway.

Finally, I thought. My hands were shaking with nervousness. Now we could get on to the inquiry.

Suddenly Owen stopped walking—about a foot from the door. "No," he said for the millionth time.

Griffin smiled tensely. "No what?" he asked.

"No," Owen said. "I want Bailey."

We all stared at him in surprise. "I want *Bailey* to take me," Owen repeated.

A huge grin spread across Bailey's face. "Okay," he said happily. "Sure—I'll take you, Owen!"

He took Owen's hand and led him out the door.

Griffin sat in Bailey's chair. We all looked at Mr. Merry.

"Can we begin?" Mr. Merry asked.

"Yes. Please," Charlie said.

"NO!" Owen's voice drifted in from the lobby.

I thought I might cry out loud. What was wrong with Owen now? Why was he acting up here, *now?*

The office door opened again, and Bailey stuck his head in. Owen followed him. "Julia—he wants *you* to take him," Bailey said quietly.

Poor Bailey. He had been so happy Owen finally wanted him instead of Julia, and now Owen was changing his mind. Bailey looked really sad.

Julia stood up and walked over to Bailey. She put her hand on his arm. "Don't worry, Bay" she whispered. "He'll get over this."

Bailey nodded.

Mr. Merry cleared his throat.

"Sorry," Julia said. She took Owen's hand and started out the door. But he stopped—again.

"Bailey!" he said.

I couldn't take it anymore. If Owen didn't stop this, these people were going to put us in a foster home just to get Owen to go to the potty!

"Owen!" I cried. "Who do you want to go with? You have to pick someone. Do you want Bailey or Julia?"

Owen's blue eyes grew wide. He stared up at Julia for a minute. Then he looked at Bailey. Then Julia again.

He's lucky he's cute, I thought. Otherwise I would be really mad at him right now.

"I want Julia," Owen said.

Bailey looked down at the ground.

"And Bailey!" Owen added.

Bailey glanced up. He and Julia grinned at each other.

"Are you *sure?*" Mr. Merry asked.

"Julia and Bailey!" Owen insisted.

Bailey jumped up and took Owen's other hand. Julia leaned over and gave Bailey a quick kiss on the cheek. "See—he still loves you," she whispered. The three of them hurried out of the office.

I caught Charlie's eye, and he gave me a relieved smile. "Let's get on with this," he said.

Mr. Merry nodded. "Good."

Then he started asking Charlie a million questions about his job, the restaurant, his past girlfriends, and even about Thurber. Charlie tried desperately to answer them.

Owen, Bailey and Julia came back and silently sat down. I felt better with all of them in the room. As if I had lots of people to protect me.

While Charlie replied to the questions, I gazed around at my family. All I could think was, I did this to them. Because of me, they're all going through this.

But then another horrible thought occurred to me.

What if this is the last time we're all together?

What if they decide to split us up and they take Owen and me *tonight?* I felt tears well up in my eyes.

Don't cry, Claudia! I ordered myself. Just hang in there. There's no way this is going to go that far. They're not going to take me away from my family.

They can't!

Just then there was another knock at the door. We all turned around to see who it was.

I gasped when I recognized her.

"Ms. Hartin!" I exclaimed.

I looked frantically at Charlie. He seemed as confused as I was. What was going on? What was *she* doing here?

Ms. Hartin walked into the office. She walked past us all, directly to Mr. Merry and Ms. Turner. She didn't even look my way.

This can't be good, I thought.

Then I realized why she was here.

To testify against Charlie!

chapter thirteen

Do you have something to add to this inquiry?" Ms. Turner asked.

"No," Ms. Hartin answered. "I'm here to withdraw my complaint against Charlie Salinger."

I almost fell off my chair. Had Ms. Hartin *really* just said those words?

Mr. Merry and Ms. Turner seemed surprised, too.

"And you are . . ." Mr. Merry asked.

"My name is Victoria Hartin. I am Claudia Salinger's English teacher." Ms. Hartin looked at me and smiled. "And I'm here to withdraw my complaint."

Charlie stood up. Julia and Griffin both gasped, and Bailey just sat there with his mouth hanging open.

I was too stunned to react. Instead, I watched Mr. Merry inspect the paperwork in front of him.

"This is unusual," he said. "On what grounds are you withdrawing your complaint, Ms. Hartin? Please remember that this office takes complaints such as yours very seriously."

Ms. Hartin nodded. "Yes. I understand," she replied. "But I had a long discussion with Claudia this morning. And I now realize that I was, well, *misinformed* when I made my complaint. Claudia explained to me this morning how things *really* work in her household. It seems I was under a false impression."

Everyone looked at me and I slouched in my chair. Okay, I thought. I deserve this.

"The situation at the Salinger home isn't nearly as bad as I thought. I spoke with some of the other teachers at the high school—teachers who've had Julia and Bailey in their classes and know their situation. They were all very supportive of Charlie and their guardian arrangement."

Charlie glanced over at me and gave me a little smile.

"The complaints I made about Charlie are not true at all," she went on. "In fact, as I've come to realize now, Claudia loves her family very much. And they love her.

It would be a tragedy to split them up. In my opinion, anyone who is responsible for raising such an intelligent teenager in a loving environment is an excellent guardian." She turned to Charlie.

"This must have been very difficult for you, Charlie," she added. "I'm so sorry to have put you in this position. I'm sorry I misjudged you."

Charlie nodded. "Thank you for saying that. And thank you for coming here."

I suddenly realized I'd been holding my breath. Slowly, I began to exhale. I looked at Mr. Merry and Ms. Turner, but their expressions hadn't changed.

Come on, I thought. You have to believe us *now!* Ms. Hartin is telling the truth.

"Mr. Merry," Bailey said. "If there's no complaint against Charlie, can we just drop this inquiry?"

Mr. Merry leaned over to whisper something to Ms. Turner. For the next three minutes, we all stood still, watching them whisper to each other. I gazed around the room. The suspense was unbearable.

Please, I prayed. Make everything work out! Don't take me away from my family. If everything works out, I promise I'll never lie again—never!

Finally, Mr. Merry stood up. I held my breath again while he spoke.

"In light of the fact that the complaint against Charles Salinger has been withdrawn, we see no reason to proceed with this inquiry. I am dismissing this case. Claudia Salinger and Owen Salinger shall remain under his custody. However, I am requesting a follow-up visit one month from today."

I exhaled loudly. I hadn't heard a thing after "I am dismissing this case." But who cares? It was all over!

I had my family back!

We all just smiled at one another. No one even moved. I didn't know whether to cry or scream or jump up and down.

So I did all three.

I ran to Charlie and threw my arms around him.

"Charlie, I'm so sorry," I said. "I promise, no matter how angry I get, I'll never, ever do anything like this again!"

Charlie hugged me even tighter. "It's okay, Claud," he said. "I'm just happy it worked out. I have to admit, though . . . I was pretty scared for a while."

I gazed up at him. "Me, too," I whispered.

Bailey carried Owen over to us and put his free arm around me. Julia and Griffin joined in on the group hug, and we stood there like one big happy family.

Sure, we must have *looked* pretty dorky, standing in a

strange office, hugging and crying like babies, but I don't think anyone cared.

"Let me out!" Owen cried, squirming to get out of the middle of our hug. "I can't breathe!"

We all laughed.

"Are you two done fighting now?" Charlie asked Julia and Bailey.

They glanced at each other and smiled.

"I guess I can get used to Julia spoiling Owen," Bailey said. "As long as he still likes me, too."

"Bay-ley!" Owen yelled.

"Oooo-wen!" Bailey yelled back.

"I think we better take this outside," Charlie joked. "Or they're going to think we're too nuts to take care of Owen."

We turned to go, but Owen stopped us.

"NO!" he yelled.

I groaned. "What is it now, Owen?" I asked.

"I want to hug again," he announced.

Even Mr. Merry chuckled.

"Okay, Owen," Charlie said, scooping my little brother into his arms. "But we might have to tickle you!"

Owen squealed with laughter as Charlie tickled

his tummy. Julia, Bailey, Griffin and I joined the hug.

Now everything is perfect again, I thought. This is the way it's supposed to be.

All of us together.

Holding on to one another for dear life.

You Could Win A Party Of Five Party In Your Own Home!

party of five ™

1 GRAND PRIZE
A "party of five" Party which will include a wide-screen TV, party provisions for the night to include pizza, ice cream and soda and "party of five" T-shirts for the winner and ten friends

5 FIRST PRIZES
"party of five" sweatshirt

15 SECOND PRIZES
"party of five" baseball hat

25 THIRD PRIZES
"party of five" T-shirt

50 FOURTH PRIZES
"party of five" mug

COLUMBIA PICTURES TELEVISION
a SONY PICTURES ENTERTAINMENT company

Complete the entry form and mail to:
Pocket Books/"party of five" Sweepstakes
Advertising and Promotion Department
1230 Avenue of the Americas
New York, NY 10020

- -

Name_____Birthdate____ /____ /_____

Address_____

City_____State_____Zip_____

Phone (_____) _____

(See next page for official rules)

Pocket Books/"party of five" Sweepstakes Official Rules:
1. No Purchase Necessary. Enter by mailing the completed Official Entry Form (no copies allowed) or by mailing on a 3" x 5" card with your name and address, daytime telephone number and birthdate to the Pocket Books/"party of five" Sweepstakes, Advertising and Promotion Department, 13th Floor, 1230 Avenue of the Americas, NY, NY 10020. Sweepstakes begins 10/7/97. Entries must be received by 3/30/98. Not responsible for lost, late, damaged, stolen, illegible, mutilated, incomplete, or misdirected or not delivered entries or mail or for typographical errors in the entry form or rules. Entries are void if they are in whole or in part illegible, incomplete or damaged. Enter as often as you wish, but each entry must be mailed separately. Winners will be selected at random from all eligible entries received in a drawing to be held on or about 4/1/98. Winners will be notified by mail.
2. Prizes: One Grand Prize: A "party of five" party which will include a wide screen TV delivered to the winner's home a few days before the season 1997-98 finale, party provisions for the evening for the winner and ten friends, which will include pizza, ice-cream and soda and "party of five" T-shirts for the winner and ten friends *(approx. retail value $2,000.00)*, Five First Prizes: "party of five" sweatshirts *(approx. retail value $30 each)* Fifteen Second Prizes: "party of five" baseball caps *(approx. retail value $16.00 each)* , Twenty-five Third Prizes: "party of five" T-shirts *(approx. retail value $15.00 each)*. Fifty Fourth Prizes: "party of five" mugs *(approx. retail value: $7.50 each)*. The Grand Prize must be taken on the dates specified by sponsors.
3. The sweepstakes is open to legal residents of the U.S. and Canada (excluding Quebec) no older than fourteen as of 3/30/98, except as set forth below. Proof of age is required to claim prize. Prizes will be awarded to the winner's parent or legal guardian. Void in Puerto Rico and wherever prohibited or restricted by law. All federal, state and local laws apply. Sony Pictures Entertainment, Inc., Columbia Pictures Television Inc., Simon & Schuster, Inc., Parachute Properties and Parachute Press, Inc. (individually and collectively "Parachute"), their respective officers, directors, shareholders, employees, suppliers, parents, subsidiaries, affiliates, agencies, sponsors, participating retailers, and persons connected with the use, marketing or conduct of this sweepstakes are not eligible. And family members living in the same household as any of the individuals referred to in the immediately forgoing sentence are not eligible.
4. One prize per person or household. Prizes are not transferable and may not be substituted except by sponsors, in the event of prize unavailability, in which case a prize of equal or greater value will be awarded. All prizes will be awarded. The odds of winning a prize depend upon the number of eligible entries received.
5. If a winner is a Canadian resident, then he/she must correctly answer a skill-based question administered by mail.
6. All expenses on receipt and use of prize including federal, state and local taxes are the sole responsibility of the winners. Winners will be notified by mail. Winners may be required to execute and return an Affidavit of Eligibility and Release and all other legal documents which the sweepstakes sponsor may require (including a W-9 tax form) within 15 days of attempted notification or an alternate winner will be selected.
7. Winners or winners' parents on winners' behalf agree to allow use of their names, photographs, likenesses, and entries for any advertising, promotion and publicity purposes without further compensation or permission from the entrants, except where prohibited by law.
8. Winners agree that Sony Pictures Entertainment Inc., Columbia Pictures Television, Inc., Simon & Schuster, Inc., Parachute, and their respective officers, directors, shareholders, employees, suppliers, parents, subsidiaries, affiliates, agencies, sponsors, participating retailers, and persons connected with the use, marketing or conduct of this sweepstakes, shall have no responsibility or liability for injuries, losses or damages of any kind in connection with the collection, acceptance or use of the prizes awarded herein, or from participation in this promotion. By participating in this sweepstakes, participants agree to release, discharge and hold harmless Sony Pictures Entertainment Inc., Columbia Pictures Television, Inc., Simon & Schuster, Inc., Parachute, and their respective officers, directors, shareholders, employees, suppliers, parents, subsidiaries, affiliates, agencies, sponsors, participating retailers, and persons connected with the use, marketing or conduct of this sweepstakes from any injuries, losses or damages of any kind arising out of the acceptance, use, misuse or possession of any prize received in this sweepstakes.
9. By participating in this sweepstakes, entrants agree to be bound by these rules and the decisions of the judges and sweepstakes sponsors, which are final in all matters relating to the sweepstakes.
10. For a list of major prize winners, (available after 4/5/98) send a stamped, self-addressed envelope to Prize Winners, Pocket Books/ "party of five" Sweepstakes, Advertising and Promotion Department, 13th Floor, 1230 Avenue of the Americas, NY, NY 10020. "party of five" and the "party of five" logo are trademarks of Columbia Pictures Television, Inc. No celebrity endorsement implied. © 1997 Columbia Pictures Television, Inc. All rights reserved.